THE UNICORN GATE

IONA JENKINS

This book is a work of fiction and any resemblance to persons
either living or dead, is purely coincidental

Front cover design from a painting by Iona Jenkins

Copyright © 2016 Iona Jenkins

ISBN: 1533653836
ISBN-13: 978-1533653833

DEDICATION

For Marley, Rohan, Nancy, Ellie, Maggie, James, Moli, Zack, Kai, Clemens, Aurelia, Leila, Elisa, Alberto, and the Magical Child in everyone..

CONTENTS

ACKNOWLEDGEMENTS

I would like to offer my thanks to Wynne for his encouragement and belief in me, to my friends in Tiny Writers for their incredible support and positive feedback, to Jan Marsh for her editing, to Dave Jones and Jan Baker for their valuable advice and help with the cover, to creative writing tutor Steven Hitchins whose patience, guidance and inspiration gave me the incentive to become a writer, to Anne Rodgers for her enthusiasm, to the courage of all the young people I worked with in my former career as a counsellor/psychotherapist and to the parks, gardens and landscapes of the British Isles which have inspired me throughout my life.
The magic is everywhere you just have to slow down and connect to feel its presence.

1 HAILSTONES

It was one of those days when the world made no sense and everything seemed pointless. Daisy Evans had begun to worry again, and when she was worried, she couldn't stop talking. Only two weeks ago she had left her old school with the promise of six whole glorious weeks of freedom but then four days later, her security had come to an abrupt end when her dad lost his job.

"I have a bit of bad news," he said looking desperate. "I'm afraid I've been made redundant. We'll all have to cut down and hope that something else turns up for me. I'm sorry Daisy but we simply can't afford to spend on outings this summer."

So, last Saturday Uncle Mark had decided to help by bringing Daisy to London for a fortnight to give his sister space to increase the small business she ran from home. Daisy thought that staying with her cousin Toby wouldn't be much of a holiday because they didn't exactly get on. Her Auntie Rosa was lovely though, "loveable but bonkers," is what her mum always said

Exactly one week later they were out on an errand to purchase a loaf of crusty bread, with Daisy nervously chattering on about this and that, unable to stop even though she knew Toby wasn't interested. Talking kept the worry away, all those crazy thoughts about what would happen if there wasn't enough money? Would she have to move? Daisy loved her home by the sea in Wales and didn't want to live anywhere else.

It was a real shame that her cousin had only inherited his mother's dark Italian looks and hadn't been blessed with her easy loveable personality. Nothing bad ever happened to Toby Malone, his life was always hunky dory and Daisy felt envious. As a matter of fact, she was certain that he didn't even like her, but then she thought cousin Toby was a just a touch nerdy because he never showed the slightest interest in the things she was passionate about such as nice clothes, music or dancing. The argument started when she decided to further his education and tell him everything she knew about her favourite boy band 'Ulterior.'

"Don't you ever shut up? You've been talking non-stop for the past ten minutes." Toby, for his part found all that gossip about people he'd never heard of difficult to cope with. It bored him to tears.

"So exactly how far are your local shops?" Daisy gave her cousin a playful push and laughed when he crashed into the high brick wall dividing the pavement from the park beyond.

"Ouch, that hurt! All your joking and messing about does my head in. Not funny Daisy, push off. I mean it!"

"You can be a teensy bit boring sometimes you know. It's so annoying I could scream!" Daisy stopped to tidy a few stray, sandy curls so that she could see clearly. Her green eyes narrowed like those of a cat as she decided to really have a go at him. "And speaking of boring, why don't you ask Auntie Rosa to get you something more cheerful to wear, something cool with some colour in it right?" She danced around him like a boxer before giving him a final not so friendly shove. Toby's brown eyes smouldered with contempt.

"You're doing it again, whenever you're here, you want me to change! It's dumb! I'm happy as I am and by the way, I don't care about stupid clothes or rubbish boy bands, so back off!" A superior expression replaced the angry frown. "Unlike some people, I don't need to be noticed all the time."

"Whatever!" Completely ignoring the suggestion that she was an attention seeker, Daisy changed the subject and proceeded to tell Toby all about the amazing secondary school she was going to in September. Toby sighed and decided to give up. He would have to cope with this for another whole week before his dad took her back to Wales.

In a sulk, he began to fasten his waterproof jacket against the unusually cold August weather. The summer had been a washout and today had brought a sharp, biting breeze with yet another dull sky overrun by scudding clouds. "Best zip up your colourful coat," Toby's tone was just on the edge of sarcastic, "it's starting to drizzle."

Daisy wasn't listening because something new and more interesting had already caught her eye. Deliberately ignoring Toby she stopped to get a better view of the statue perched above her. A reclining white stone unicorn stretched out across the top of the wall, as though it had been put there to protect the green door below with its peeling paint and scrawling graffiti. Set back from the pavement in a grey granite surround, the unused entrance had a shabby, neglected air.

"I never noticed that statue on my last visit," she sounded, surprised.

"It's always been there," replied Toby, his mood changing along with the subject of the conversation. "Pity it's too big for my mother's collection, I ask you — the woman has an entire shelf of pottery unicorns with embarrassing names like Star and Rainbow. Strictly un-cool! This one must have been put there to guard that doorway," he added in a mocking tone.

"So what's to guard?" asked Daisy with some impatience.

"Oh I don't know, the portal to an alien dimension maybe?"

"Now you really have lost it!"

" It's a joke!" He was laughing at her again.

"Yes well … as we know, there's only a stupid park over the wall, and this is a skanky old door. Still, I expect Auntie Rosa has got a dippy name for it. The unicorn I mean!" Daisy's tone was teasing again as she began rattling the worn metal doorknob, trying to twist it open. "Look, it's locked."

As she spoke, a freak blast of cold air arriving out of the blue, forced them to pull on their hoods to protect their ears. An advancing army of dense black clouds moved in as a peal of thunder like a war drum and a bolt of forked lightning shattered the heavy sky. Hailstones! It was like being pelted with a million pebbles. The storm became so fierce they were obliged to squeeze into the shallow stone recess, pressing their faces against the green door in a hopeless attempt to secure some protection from the noisy stinging hail battering the pavement and the line of parked cars.

Then, without the slightest warning, the door was blown wide open, hurling both of them into the green space beyond before slamming shut with one very final deafening thud. Toby's realization of being unhurt and lying on soft dry earth where there should have been a tarmac path came on gradually as the shock of being thrown into the air subsided. *There are far too many trees here and no evidence at all of any door, statue or boundary wall,* he thought to himself, *I don't understand!* Uneasy and puzzled by the unfamiliar surroundings, he sat bolt up-right, discovering with relief that Daisy was also uninjured, very conscious and sitting up only a few feet away from him.

"Daise," he gasped. "Something really wild's happening. This isn't the park... and the storm's over."

"Tell me about it! " The girl began brushing some stray grains of earth from her scarlet anorak and best skinny jeans. The ground beneath her was perfectly dry, with tufts of fresh green grass and bluebells as far as she could see.

"Look at these flowers Toby. Something's not normal, it's actually August, I mean like late summer, and bluebells always grow in early May. At home, I often go out walking with my Mum so I know. This is seriously weird."

Toby clambered to his feet and took a good long look around him. "I'm afraid I don't know very much about flowers but I am sure I've never seen this place before, and it certainly has nothing to do with the park near my house. This isn't logical! Where are we?"

"Right ... we're in a clearing," Daisy decided, trying to get her bearings. "We appear to be in the middle of a forest ... there are several narrow paths leading in different directions through the trees ... Unfortunately, though, the wall and that door with the statue have actually vanished ... there's crazy ... but the bonus is that there's tons of bluebells like carpets all over the place and it smells really lush."

"That's okay then, Daisy likes the smell!" Toby, sensible as ever, pulled his new phone from the pocket of his charcoal grey waterproof. "I may not be exactly what you want, but I'm always practical even in situations as alarming as this one. It's cool. I'll call home and tell Mum and Dad what's happened and I'm sure they'll be able to come up with some kind of solution." Toby's face registered shock. " Useless - there's no signal. My smart phone is a complete waste of space in this weird forest. What about yours, Daise?" he asked, trying hard not to panic.

Daisy scowled. "I'm afraid not, mine's dead too. No sensible Uncle Mark to help, then. Looks like we've got a serious problem."

Returning the phone to his pocket, Toby pulled off his hood. "So, what now? ... Nobody older to take over and sort things out and damn - my watch has packed up as well. Why doesn't anything work in this dumb place? I remember noticing it was eleven o'clock just before the hailstorm and now it feels like late afternoon, not to mention that it's become spring all of a sudden and grown acres of minging bluebells." His fear was rapidly turning into irritation.

"Perhaps it's really the middle of the night and one of us is dreaming." Daisy suggested, trying to convince herself, that none of it was really happening.

"No chance, I distinctly remember getting up this morning and everything else between then and trying to shelter from the hail."

"You would!" Then she realized they were no longer alone.

"Over there! Looks like a white horse. Wonder if it's lost same as us?" Daisy was leaping up and down, pointing into the trees behind Toby, who had to spin around to see why she was so agitated. Under a broad oak on the edge of one of the bluebell lined paths stood a shimmering white horse surrounded by an eerie pocket of hovering mist, its appearance ghostly, almost transparent. Then as Toby focused on the apparition, it materialized completely and became as solid as he was.

"I'm not very sure that's a horse Daise ... Nah... It's impossible... it's awesome, there's a horn in the middle of its head ... there's no such thing... this is nuts!" Toby sounded startled. "I swear it's a unicorn!"

The animal had stepped out of its spooky cloak of mist, which promptly dissolved in a convenient ray of sunlight forging its way through the canopy of leaves. As the creature turned to face them, the spiral horn jutting from the centre of its forehead sent sparks of golden light, cascading over its head and down the length of its mane. Daisy didn't feel like cracking any jokes about her Auntie Rosa giving it a name because, for once in her colourful life, she was speechless.

2 THROUGH THE FOREST

"Crazy or not, that white horse has got to be a unicorn, I mean you can't really argue with the horn sticking out of its head can you?" Daisy approached the creature with some caution. "Come on Toby, don't just stand there looking pathetic. There's no way to avoid this, so our only choice is to check it out. I've never heard of any aggressive unicorns so we should be okay and anyway, it appears to have something to say and maybe it can tell us how to get out of here."

They could both hear the animal speaking though it never once opened its mouth. There was no voice in the normal sense, but somehow in individual ways, they were both listening to a conversation. What Toby heard was delivered in a tone like silver bells, whilst Daisy imagined musical notes, flashing in a variety of vibrant hues like disco lights. No longer afraid, their only immediate desire was to move in closer and hear whatever the magical beast had to tell them.

"At last I've found you!" The creature sounded enthusiastic and even spoke English. "Welcome to Lumenor."

"Lumenor?" shrieked Daisy, somewhat taken aback. "Lumenor? "Are you sure? Whatever happened to the stupid park on the other side of that green door? What on earth is Lumenor? We're supposed to be going to the shop to buy some crusty bread for lunch so we have to be on our way, right, and I mean now!"

"Ah," replied the unicorn, "that is all very well, but you have fallen through a doorway in the storm and regardless of lunch or anything else, you are definitely supposed to be here. I have seen it written in the stars and in the records of the universe. I have been waiting for you, because now is the right time and you are the right people. It is a matter of a little thing called destiny and you cannot avoid it."

"I haven't the slightest idea what you're talking about," said an overwhelmed Toby. "As far as I'm concerned this is crazy stuff. We're supposed to be on an errand right now and the only thing that's helping me to cope is the fact that my mother happens to love unicorns. Do you have a name by the way? I always prefer to know who I'm talking to."

"Of course," the voice went on, in silver bells and disco colours. "However, since the name in my own language would be a chore for you to pronounce, you can call me Rio because that's easy to remember."

"Thanks a bunch! And what about this place then? Lumenor seems to be an enormous wood."

"Well," answered Rio, "you are not exactly in Lumenor yet, you have to take the correct path. This is the Dreaming Forest. People can wander around in here for years, you know, until they go mad, there are so many pathways leading to dead ends or just going round and round in circles. Some people come here in dreams - they get in by accident. It really keeps me busy seeking them out and sending them home."

"Sounds more like nightmares to me." Daisy was anxiously twisting a lock of hair and wishing that the unicorn would decide to send her home.

"There is no problem for you," said Rio in calming pale blues and pinks, which were meant to soothe Daisy's irritation. "It is impossible for you to be lost, because you were sent here for a particular reason and besides, I am your personal guide. As I previously explained, I have been waiting for you, but it is getting late and we have to be at the edge of the forest at least a couple of hours before dusk, so we had better get moving."

Toby and Daisy gave up fretting about the bread or the whereabouts of the green door because there was no further chance that it could ever be found. With no more options or choices to be had, they removed their jackets in the warm temperature of the sheltered woodland, and tying the sleeves around their waists followed Rio down one of the many paths, twisting and turning far away into the depths of the forest towards an unknown destination.

Warmed by the late afternoon sun filtering through the leaves, and the sweet scent of bluebells, walking became so pleasant and relaxing that they hardly noticed the time passing. They both felt more energetic in this dreamy place so alive with spring flowers and birdsong, they could have walked for hours with their new companion.

All too soon, Rio stopped abruptly, turning his head to face his young companions. "So, we are here at last, the Gate into Lumenor."

The trees had thinned to reveal a low, wooden fence with a gate where the path came to an end. Sturdy and unpainted, the gate looked quite ordinary except that it opened by itself as Rio approached, almost as though it was alive and recognized him. One by one, they stepped out onto the brow of a grassy knoll where a trio of fluttering larks whistled a tune of welcome in a pale blue sky. Below them a white thatched cottage sat snugly in its own green enclosure at the base of the hill.

"Apart from the obvious change in season from summer to spring," said Toby this could be a countryside view anywhere in the British Isles – well that is if we hadn't recently crossed over into some mysterious place called Lumenor."

Rio glanced at the sun. "We have made good time, so you can take it slowly if you like. Morag, the woman, who lives in that house down there, belongs to an ancient order whose members have long been the guardians of this Land, a group of people known as the Order of Lumen. Take my advice and trust her completely."

"Aren't you coming with us?" asked Daisy, not wanting to lose their guide in a place about which she knew nothing at all.

"No," the creature replied. "I am merely responsible for entrances and exits between worlds, your guide through the Dreaming Forest. You have opened a Unicorn Gate, thus allowing me to bring you here at a time when your own destiny is in direct alignment with the destiny of Lumenor. You need to be on your way now and I must return into the forest to rescue a small group of silly daydreamers who must be sent home at once."

Rio touched each of the children on the forehead with the tip of his horn and then he was gone. The wooden gate had already closed and the creature had vanished into thin air. All that remained were sparks of golden light falling on to their shoulders and some words, which seemed strangely like a memory from long ago echoing through both their minds.

The Mist, surround and protect you.
The Earth, support and nourish you
The Sun, warm your heart with laughter
The Moon, light your way in darkness
The stars come down and sing to you.

They looked at each other, repeating the words in unison before bursting into a bout of nervous laughter, because they had both heard the same strange verse at the same time. For a moment, they were stunned and unable to move.

"What's all that about then?" Daisy recovered first as a big smirk spread across her face "Race you,'" she yelled, giving Toby yet another sharp shove. Recovering his balance, he ran down the hill in pursuit. "Hey, Evans, I hope this person Morag, whoever she is, has enough patience to put up with you!"

The odd thing was that, when they reached the bottom of the slope and looked back, there was no sign that the Dreaming Forest had ever existed. All that remained was a small cluster of Scots pines, tall sentinels standing on the brow of the hill with the mild west wind singing through their branches like a forgotten melody played on harp strings. There really was no way back and without a gate, a guide and the Dreaming Forest, the only available choice for Toby and Daisy was to head towards the white cottage in search of someone called Morag.

3 MORAG

The back gate leading through the hedge into the cottage garden bore a striking resemblance to the one at the forest's edge in the way it opened by itself.

"Looks like we really are expected then," Daisy observed entering the garden.

Following the obvious direction of a flower-bordered path leading towards the house, they crossed a small orchard of fruit trees, resplendent with pink and white blossoms and a spring green lawn opening out at the rear of the cottage. There was a row of buzzing beehives, a vegetable patch and an assortment of earthenware pots containing fragrant herbs.

"It's lovely here and I feel safe." Daisy walked off leaving Toby alone.

As Toby's confidence returned, all his previous uncertainty dissolved, and a sense of expectation began to awaken.

"I don't care now about the bread or what time it is," he said out loud, this adventure really livens up an annoying summer holiday I've been forced to spend with crazy Daisy."

Lucky for him, Daisy didn't hear the insult because she was fully engaged in her own exploration of the garden and had just that minute discovered an enormous silver lantern decorated with flowers and leaves skillfully crafted from golden metal. Positioned on a low white pillar not far from the back door, its beauty held her attention for a full two minutes as she stood wondering whether or not those leaves were made of real gold.

"You have to come and get a look at this Toby," she called with excitement, "it's epic."

"Wow!" Toby was intrigued, "there's a brilliant carved crystal at the centre. You'd expect to see either a bulb or a candle there wouldn't you? I can't see any wires so I'm baffled as to how it could possibly work as a light."

"You're right - but whoever made this, must have been some sort of special craftsman. I've never seen anything like it back home. I know you were joking earlier, but it looks as if the door, I mean the Unicorn Gate, was a portal to an alien dimension after all," she turned her attention back to the curious lantern. "What did Rio call this place again?" "Lumenor."

"Yeah, that's it, Lumenor, though except for this lantern … the dimension doesn't look very alien does it?"

Caught up in the lantern's spell, they were unaware of the door opening until a pleasant female voice broke the silence.

"You're here are at last – the young people described in an obscure golden harp prophecy, discovered after such a long and desperate search."

Framed by the open door way, the slender silver haired woman simply clothed in an elegant long dress of watery green silk resembled a figure from a mediaeval painting. Around her neck hung an unusual knot work pendant set with a single, milky gem. Her fingers were adorned with delicate rings and a plaited silver belt outlined her waist. Daisy thought she looked both old and young at the same time. It was impossible to guess her age.

"Hiya, I'm Daisy and this is my cousin Toby," she said with a wary glance towards the enormous untidy grey dog standing beside the woman.

The dog held Toby captive in a steady gaze, almost as if he were sizing him up. Eventually, the animal blinked and wagged his tail, leaving Toby with the impression that he had passed some kind of test.

"Cool - the dog approves and says I can stay … Wait a minute, how do I know that?"

"Of course he approves, why wouldn't he? I am Morag and I can't tell you just how glad I am that you're finally here." The woman's voice was light and melodic. "And this is Finn, he's a wolfhound but also my friend and protector. Welcome to our home. I've been making a careful study of the heavens and listening to the Lumerin these past two days because I knew your arrival was imminent."

"What exactly are the Lumerin?" inquired Toby, eagerly following Morag into the tiled hallway of the traditional beamed cottage. Daisy kept her mouth shut. Somehow, Morag's presence had caused feelings of shyness, which for her was an entirely new experience.

"All in good time, but first, hang your coats on the hall stand, I have prepared refreshments, I hope you're hungry."

The white interior walls of the cottage set off the stained, dark wooden beams and natural slate floors. Four floral armchairs surrounded a stone inglenook fireplace containing a pile of logs, which had not yet been lit. On a low, wooden table, Morag had laid out a small feast of chunky brown bread, cheese, fruit and honey from her own bees. A jug of fresh apple juice was waiting to be poured into the rustic stoneware goblets.

"Help yourself." Morag disappeared into the kitchen in search of butter and a wicked looking chocolate cake.

"It's odd Daise, have you noticed how there's no television or any kind of modern technology in this sitting room. I can't see a PC or a tablet."

"You're absolutely right but there's some other weird old things over in that corner. This place is so not now."

A heavy grey metal typewriter occupied the centre of a mahogany desk, next to a notebook and an ugly big black telephone, which had a huge chrome dial for composing numbers. "Must be antiques," Toby said without bothering to comment further, because he was hungry and eager to get close to the food.

"This crockery reminds me of stuff from a Welsh pottery not far from my home," observed Daisy, picking up a plate before helping herself to a thick slice of cheese and the biggest chunk of bread in the basket.

Morag's deep blue eyes glittered like sapphires as she placed the chocolate cake on the table and cut them a piece each. "Ah, Lumenor is a bit like that you know, you're often reminded of things you've seen before."

"Like you remind me of the moon, Morag," Toby was thoughtful. "Anyway, what's the info on this harp thing we're supposed to be in?"

Morag's expression became very serious. "It's written that two young ones, a boy and a girl, will open a doorway from a faraway world. He is a Communicator - one who can speak with all living things - and she is a Healer of Souls - one who can mend hurt and still fear. They will come to us in a time when dark intentions threaten the stability of our Land. The lost will be found and the golden Harp of Creation will sing again in the Hall of Awen, bringing peace harmony and wonderful inspiration to Lumenor and to all who can hear it's song."

"You're joking right!" yelled Daisy, almost dropping her plate. "Tell me it's a joke. You can't seriously believe that's got anything to do with us. I mean we're just a couple of kids right and we're starting secondary school in September so there's no chance at all of us getting involved. I'm only staying with my cousin because my dad's been made redundant and my parents, need a bit of space to sort out their problems. I never intended to get into some mental place called Lumenor or of being a Healer of Souls, whatever you think. This is really rubbish and I'm well upset." Daisy was fuming as hot tears seeped from the corner of her eyes. "It's so unfair! My life's never going to be normal again, I want to go home!"

Toby, a little shocked at his cousin's extreme response, was on the verge of telling Daisy to chill, but on second thoughts decided it might only cause more trouble. For the first time since her arrival in London, he saw how worried and anxious

Daisy was and even more surprisingly he became aware that he actually cared about her; she was family after all, even if she was sometimes totally annoying. He wished he'd shown her a little more understanding.

Morag glanced kindly at the girl, but then continued to speak, taking hold of Daisy's hand in a sympathetic manner designed to reassure, and discourage any further bitter outbursts. "I don't think it's you," she stated with absolute certainty. "I know it's you. I belong to a group of people called the Order of Lumen. It's our job to know these things because we have long been the guardians of this world."

Daisy calmed down as Morag suddenly began to take on a far greater importance. They could both see that their host was not some delicate woman in fancy dress, but a very substantial person with deep knowledge and purpose in this world of Lumenor, where they were strangers. The truth is that they were very much in awe of this new friend who certainly commanded respect.

Morag smiled warmly and the atmosphere softened. "Finish your chocolate cake. The day is fading fast into that magical time of twilight when the veil between worlds thins and anything is possible. This is when we seek to call the Lumerin, so if you would care to follow me into the garden and take your places around the lantern, then I'm sure you will begin to understand."

4 THE LUMERIN

In the garden, a blackbird piped a sweet end to daylight as the still air of twilight wrapped them gently in its magic cloak. At this hour, as day began to creep into night, Toby had the feeling that his part in deciding the fate of Lumenor was a sealed deal whether he liked it or not.

The cousins joined Morag and Finn outside, standing in a semi-circle before the great lantern. A very bright group of stars had risen in the darkening sky, close to the sharp crescent of a new moon as Morag began to sing an entrancing melody in a high, clear voice. Daisy had no idea what the words meant, but just like that strange verse, they sounded sort of familiar again, like something she had heard in a dream long ago… something she ought to remember…

A beam of light began to stream from the centre of the bright constellation in response to Morag's song. The children stepped back as it grew wider and wider, heading for the lantern in front of them. The shapes of beautiful people became visible, floating, smiling and singing back to Morag. Then, the light formed itself into a ball, hitting the lantern full on, igniting the crystal like a bulb, only much brighter than anything electrical. As the choral singing faded, the glow from the crystal spread out, illuminating the garden and chasing shadows.

Morag was speaking now, still using that same language, and, in response, a sweet chorus echoed back from the crystal in the lantern, as though she had asked a question and it was being answered.

"The Lumerin are here!" she exclaimed joyfully at the end of the conversation. "So, now I should tell you about them."

In the cottage Morag lit the fire and brought a pot of tea to the table. Finn lay dozing on the hearth with his head on his paws, enjoying the warmth and Toby was now very impatient to understand exactly what he had just witnessed.

"There are aliens here Daisy, the Lumerin are aliens."

"So are we Toby."

"Yes, but these Lumerin are awesome, I could never have imagined such a thing. It was so good out there, like I was being wrapped in a blanket of kindness."

"And so you were," replied Morag, settling back in her armchair to begin her tale.

"Long ago, there were two races inhabiting Lumenor. One human and the other a people called Lumerin, who originally came from a distant constellation of stars. They lived in harmony side by side with the human race, helping them to evolve by passing on their wonderful wisdom and knowledge. The Lumerin cared so much for the humans that some of them intermarried and had children. These descendants were sensitive and creative, many with gifts of second sight and healing. All of them had their own unique talents, which they loved to share.

"Others of the Lumerin became so bright, they no longer needed bodies, and so passed into another, lighter dimension. Eventually, memories of them faded over many generations as people lost interest. It was as though a spell had been cast over the population, as if they had been lulled into a deep sleep. And so, the Lumerin became the stuff of fairy tales, told only to children at bedtime."

"That's such a shame, they don't know what they're missing." Toby was sad for the terrible loss of something so beautiful.

"The Order of Lumen was formed by those who

remembered their origins, to preserve and pass on that knowledge, along with ceremonies and songs associated with those wonderful beings. In our role as guardians, we have done what we can for the people of Lumenor, though more and more, we too are becoming as legendary as the Lumerin. Known only to each other, we make our way in this world, living in harmony with it and using our gifts to help wherever and whenever we can.

"The Lumerin are called at twilight in the language of Ancient Lumen, which was once spoken by all the people. Lanterns, like the one in my garden enable us to maintain some of their light, but unfortunately, a number of our crystals have lately been corrupted and turned black."

"What do you mean by corrupted?" asked Daisy, who in spite of all her former objections was becoming interested in the story.

"Some years ago, one of our Order travelled across the Northern Ocean and there on the barren Island of Storms, he found ancient texts, which enabled him to form a connection to a dark star, a star in a frozen dimension ruled by cruelty and greed. From these beings, he learned a very different song, calling terrible shadows into Lumenor.

"In mid Earthstill of the previous year, Maxwell Delano, for that is his name, went to the central meeting place of our Order on Ynys Yr Delyn, an island in the western sea. There, in the Hall of Awen, stands a golden harp, which when played by a high harpist, radiates the special qualities of our Lumerin to all who are open enough to feel its influence. In the centre at the apex of this harp, sits the Heart of Stars, a priceless, clear jewel empowered with the music of the Great Song from which all things are formed."

"You mentioned something called Earthstill Morag, what is that?"

"Our calendar year has four seasons; we are now in Floria, the next is Greening then Treefall and finally Earthstill. The year has three hundred and sixty days divided into four seasons of ninety days each. The first day of each season goes back to one, so today, for example is the forty-eighth day of Floria and the first day of next year will be the twelfth day of Earthstill which also known as Threshold. We are now in the year 2204, calculated from the arrival of the first Lumerin."

"Wow, complicated or what Toby?"

"Easy peasy! Carry on with the story Morag."

"There are also seven other jewels, set in a row down the front frame below the Heart of Stars. Because Delano stole the greatest jewel, the Order of Lumen removed the seven, hiding each one in a secret location. We are afraid that Maxwell Delano may link our Heart to his Dark Star and that the gentle land we love will be filled with despair and eventually destroyed."

"This Delano is only one person, though," ventured Toby, looking hopeful. "Surely, there's enough of your Order of Lumen to finish him. I mean, you have all that light from your Lumerin."

Morag, who had begun to look like she was carrying the weight of the whole world replied, "It is unfortunate, but Maxwell has managed to convince many people that his way is right. There has been enough time for his influence to seep into Lumenor, spreading like a virus, because we did too little in the beginning, believing that he could not possibly interfere with the Lumerin. Only when the Heart of Stars disappeared and it was too late did we take the threat seriously and begin to look for a solution in our vast libraries. It was fortunate that we were able to discover the old prophecy but we have also learned a hard lesson from paying too little attention to protecting our treasure. There is a way forward now though the outcome cannot be guaranteed."

"I'm sorry, but what can we possibly do about all that?" Daisy demanded, getting grumpy again. "It's gruesome!"

"The Order of Lumen has been largely forgotten and the Lumerin have passed into legend. However, according to the prophecy, you are destined to help us and that is why you have been sent here."

"I still don't see what it's got to do with me!" Daisy looked miserable because she had no control over this situation.

"You have been sent to track down the seven jewels, steal back the Heart of Stars, and defeat Maxwell Delano before he can find an incantation potent enough to turn it black and bend it to the destructive will of Dark Star. I know he has not yet succeeded because the Lumerin who are attuned to its energy have told me so." Morag stopped to look directly at the two incredulous young people.

"It's gobsmacking!" Toby exclaimed. "D'you really think that two kids like me and Daise can do that?" The feelings of possibility from the lantern ceremony at twilight were rapidly disappearing.

A noise outside put an end to any further questions. Shouting, swearing and commotion streamed in through the half-open window. Finn leapt to his feet, growling. When Morag opened the door, he bounded out in a fury, snarling and barking as he hurled himself towards the front gate leading out towards the road on the other side of the orchard. The unfortunate youths, who had tried to break it down when it refused to open, ran away in terror. What they heard sounded more like a ferocious wild animal, than a dog. That was one of Finn's special talents.

"They come from the town of Robinswood," said Morag. "They've probably been drinking something intoxicating and are looking for places to steal valuables and vandalize. The worst possibility is that they could be direct followers of Maxwell Delano, though I think that's unlikely. It's time to ask the Lumerin to help me to create a stronger protection for the boundary. Tonight I have realized the necessity to conceal this place from anyone who has no connection to our Order. This time I will not delay."

Daisy didn't want to leave the safety of Morag's cottage and the magic of the Lumerin, but she had to ask Morag the question she had been dreading.

"When do we have to go?"

21

"Tomorrow, early, when Jacob from the farm across the road comes to collect you. In the town of Robinswood, you will find Gabriel Greenway. People think that Gabriel's a herbalist, a manufacturer of plant remedies and scented bath-time products, which in fact is true, but I can assure you he's much more than that. Gabriel has been chosen to share this difficult destiny."

"Mega brilliant, can't tell you what a relief it is there'll be someone older to help us get through all this." Toby's spirits lifted at the thought of company.

"I suppose we'll have to ask for directions, as we've never been to Robinswood before." Daisy sounded irritable.

"Don't speak to anyone," advised Morag urgently. "I'm serious! The longer we can keep you a secret the better. I'm worried that Delano has information about our Harp Prophecy and that he could already be aware of your arrival in Lumenor."

"Have you got a map, then?" asked Daisy sarcastically, wondering how she was going to find this Gabriel in a strange town without the help of the Internet and her phone.

Morag gave her a stern glance, but continued giving instructions and ignoring Daisy's latest tone of voice.

"A guide will show you the way. Toby, you will be able to recognize this guide - who may not be a human - so keep your wits about you. Just remember that you can communicate with all living things."

"If you say so," stammered Toby, still unsure about that but willing to accept Morag's instructions without question now.

The fire collapsed into the grate.

"Bedtime for you two!" Morag was already heading towards the staircase.

"I'm not going to argue with you Morag," grumbled Daisy, "I'm totally exhausted and well stressed about all of this but what can you do in such circumstances?"

"Just one more thing, Morag. How did the Lumerin travel so quickly from a constellation of stars that must be physically light years away?" Toby asked.

"Through a portal between their dimension and ours."

" You mean a Unicorn Gate! That's how we got here."

Morag nodded, smiling, " Never forget Toby, it is love that opens the right doors."

On the landing they were shown two identical bedrooms and an old fashioned bathroom, which Toby described as a museum exhibit. There wasn't even a shower over the cast iron bath, let alone a shower cubicle. And what about that chain for flushing the toilet! Neatly folded cotton pyjamas in exactly the right sizes had been placed on each starched white pillow and the curtains had been drawn.

Daisy fell asleep almost immediately, dreaming she was surrounded by delicate shades of colour and that the stars were still singing. As she listened to the song, the colours seemed to expand into a space within, radiating from her outstretched hands in rainbow rays. She wondered what would happen if she touched someone.

Toby took a little longer to fall asleep, not just because the wool blankets and starched sheets felt so different from his duvet, but also because his mind refused to stop churning over what he had just learned about the Harp of Creation, the Lumerin and, of course, Maxwell Delano. Thinking about Maxwell Delano made him cold and scared, filling his room with shadows and vague mutterings he did not want to hear.

Eventually exhausted, he drifted into a wonderful dream. In the garden, Toby was deep in conversation with an exceptionally tall, bright lady whose transparent form was of a shimmering, pale, golden light. Although she spoke in the same foreign language he had heard earlier, Toby thought that he had understood everything she told him, though he was unable to remember a single word of it when he awoke. There was a tremendous feeling of safety in her presence. And so, the two destined Children of the Harp slept and dreamed on into the early morning.

5 ROBINSWOOD

Toby and Daisy ate a breakfast of porridge and honey, washing it down with mugs of tea, whilst Finn padded around the kitchen waiting for Morag to feed him.

"This kitchen's very surprising, Morag." Daisy couldn't help herself. "You don't have a microwave, a dishwasher or tumble drier, the fridge has a very rounded door and I've never seen a cooker like that or a washer with rollers for wringing water out of the laundry. You really don't have a computer, mobile or even a telly do you?"

"And here's me thinking I had all the very latest. I must say that more and more people do seem to be getting televisions these days but I don't want one myself. I always have plenty to do." Morag laughed.

Daisy blushed, hoping that her new friend did not think her impolite, but the whole thing seemed a bit rubbish and just as ancient as the bathroom. She stared at the wooden radio, from which a man was crooning about his lost girlfriend. It was becoming apparent that Lumenor existed in a totally different time frame and as that ruled out the possibility of texting anyone, how could she possibly cope?

This morning Morag looked quite different with her hair tied back in a single thick plait. Dressed in a fawn skirt and cream shirt, she obviously had more ordinary things to do during the day, which didn't involve gliding around in silk and silver.

When the old kitchen clock chimed eight, Morag was keen for them to finish up to be outside for eight-thirty. Two identical green canvas rucksacks stood in readiness by the door.

"I've packed two changes of clothes each and warm knitted jackets as well as torches and a few emergency chocolate supplies. Daisy, pass me your bright red waterproof... it will need to be changed."

Mystified, Daisy handed over the jacket, wondering how that could possibly happen. Laying the garment on the floor, Morag passed both her hands over it three times. The red began to darken until it finally became the deepest green of a dense pine forest.

Daisy stared at it in disbelief. "My beautiful scarlet!" she exclaimed in some distress. "It's turned into a tedious Toby coat. How rubbish is that?"

"I know you like bright colours, Daisy," soothed Morag, passing her hands over the skinny indigo jeans, blue top and red trainers Daisy was already wearing, "but you need to be hidden as much as possible. It doesn't matter in the slightest, you know, because the colours are really inside you and the clothes you choose are just your way of expressing that."

Daisy looked at her favourite, butterfly tunic and skinny jeans, which were quickly turning into an earthy shade. "Oh well, I suppose," she sighed, "I guess I'd prefer to be safe, so I'm going to trust your judgement, as you obviously know better than I do what's going on in this screwed-up place. I also have to admit that what you did is some kind of magic."

Secretly, Daisy wondered what else her new friend was capable of, but didn't dare ask.

Morag turned to look through the window. She knew that there was precious little safety now in Lumenor, and if that prophecy failed, it was unlikely that anybody would ever be secure again. The children were lively this morning, but she knew that their road would hold both danger and darkness. Maxwell Delano was no stranger to her and, right at that moment, she wished with all her heart that he had never been born. Finn's damp nose, nuzzling Morag's hand, brought her back to the morning's urgent business.

"Come, it's time to leave," she announced, handing each of them a rucksack before leading the way through the front door and then out towards the road where a shabby, black car was already waiting. Toby, who knew a lot about cars from information on the Internet, decided it had to be an old Morris Oxford.

After saying their goodbyes, Toby and Daisy climbed into the back seat. Daisy, a little emotional and scared to leave her cozy haven with Morag and Finn, brushed away a tear as they drove away. Toby on the other hand was really hooked by the new situation, taken aback at the sight of so many old, classic cars passing by on the other side of the road. Many of them, looked brand new. He spotted a Ford Anglia, a Vauxhall Victor, an Austin van and a modest Morris 1000. *What if we've gone back to a time when our grandparents were our age?* Toby thought. It's going to be very different. Considering the cars and his experience of Morag's cottage, he decided that Lumenor was definitely stuck in a time warp. There was, a variety of familiar things, but not necessarily things from the twenty first century. *No wonder my phone doesn't work. It hasn't been invented. How will I cope without it?* Suddenly forgetting the cars, he experienced a momentary sense of loss. Ah well, that's how things are so I guess I'll just have to put up and shut up.

Daisy, deep in thought, took little notice of the passing scenery. "Who knows what happens now," she murmured to herself, settling back in her unfamiliar clothes, wondering if the two outfits in the rucksack were also dark green and brown and what her best friend Katy Davies would think when there were no more texts.

Jacob, their plump, balding chauffeur, was a cheerful type. Driving rather fast, he kept on talking all the way to Robinswood, where he pulled up outside an inn called The Black Bull and pointed down the narrow street, running alongside the river to the left of the inn.

"Just you follow that lane until you come to the bridge. Cross the river and then wait by the bushes on the bank. Someone will come for you. Best keep away from the main road as there are lots of people around at this time of day, and you don't know whom you might meet. I hope, my young friends, that we may see each other again, but in better circumstances." And so, Jacob drove away, leaving the cousins feeling both lost and apprehensive.

* * * *

At the same time as Toby and Daisy were getting out of the car, dubious odd job man Sid Planks, a tall, skinny, individual with combed back greasy hair and overalls, came out of the Black Bull to get a step ladder from his van. He was just about to begin some painting he had been hired to do in the landlord's upstairs flat, when he noticed them. It was curious, because only last week he had begun attending a series of meetings in the Town Hall, where a crowd of people were gathering to hear some new ideas an important bloke called Maxwell Delano was spreading around.

He'd been listening to one of Delano's top associates Irina Slack, who had said, "You can achieve great power over other people and get whatever you want by following the Way of the Dark Star." Sid was keen on the idea of a dark star because he was a bully who liked pushing others around and anything that gave him an excuse to do that, in addition to getting whatever he wanted, had to be a good bet in his otherwise routine life.

Spotting the two young ones, he thought this Irina woman might well be interested, as she had asked everyone at the meeting to report any newcomers and especially newcomer kids to her as soon as possible. She was obviously high up in the Dark Star organization and he might get a reward for turning them in. He remembered that he had a card with her phone number in his wallet.

As soon as Toby and Daisy entered the lane by the inn, Sid leapt after them, roughly grabbing Daisy's arm.

"What's in them bags, then?" His demand was menacing. "And where d'you think yer off to, eh?"

"Get your hands off me, you revolting creep!" Daisy struggled to break free, the fear in her stomach sending adrenaline rushing around her body. The fright turned rapidly into anger as she leaned forward, sinking her teeth into the unsavoury flesh of the man's skinny hand and biting as hard as she could.

"You little..."As Planks yelped and swore, instinctively bringing his injured hand up to his mouth to lick the wound, Toby kicked him in the right shin with a force that sent Sid crashing into the wall of the inn.

"YES!" Toby was elated. "Run for it, Daise!" he screamed, sprinting off along the lane as fast as he could. Fully recovered now, Daisy followed hot on his heels, glancing behind, expecting to see the man in pursuit but the lane was empty. Sid Planks had twisted his bony ankle when he fell and was still sprawling on the ground, cursing loudly and shouting threats.

Reaching the bridge, the cousins crossed the water and hid in the bushes on the opposite bank, huddling together as they tried to recover from the shock of their nasty encounter.

"Hope the guide comes very soon..." Daisy was hot from running but breathing easily.

Toby, who had begun to think about Maxwell Delano again, was unusually cold and shaky. Sensing his discomfort, Daisy instinctively put her hands on his shoulders and as she did so, saw a silvery blue colour coming from her fingers. Toby calmed down and warmed up.

"What did you just do?" he asked, completely surprised.

"Not sure, you were shaking and some pale blue light came from my fingers."

"Healer of Souls?" ventured Toby. "You know, the Harp Prophecy thing yeah! Maybe this is what a Healer of Souls can do. I've stopped shaking and that awful jittery feeling is going away."

"There's tidy!" Daisy shrugged and examined both her hands. "The colour's gone now. We'll know if I can do it again another time."

They only noticed the smooth black cat when it started rubbing against Toby's leg. Stroking the silken fur, he got the idea that the cat was called Midnight and that they were supposed to follow it.

"Are you crazy?" Daisy sneered at his suggestion.

"No! You are not crazy." Toby could hear the voice of the indignant cat in his mind, "but she obviously is! Are you ready or not? I do not have the time to be arguing or sitting around, and neither do you, because something bad has already happened."

"How do you know?" Toby eyed the cat with suspicion.

"I am a cat," she purred. "I know all sorts. Humans think that we animals do not have much of a brain, but they have no idea. I am different to humans, but certainly not less intelligent. Anyway, Gabriel Greenway is waiting and he does not have much time, either, because the plans have already been made."

At the mention of Gabriel, Toby was on his feet.

"Come on, Daisy. She's definitely the guide because she knows someone called Gabriel Greenway. Her name's Midnight, by the way."

Daisy's respect for Toby increased tenfold as some insight into his ability began to dawn on her. She jumped up, ready to follow the cat.

You're obviously communicating with all living things, Toby, including black cats called Midnight. Hope she's lucky for us. Just as well you went to martial arts classes."

"Just as well you've got teeth like a vampire," answered Toby, laughing as he gave Daisy a playful prod. "The greasy sad dork has obviously given up and gone home."

Without knowing just how mistaken they were, the cousins followed the cat into the streets of lower Robinswood.

* * * *

When Sid Planks finally managed to scrape himself off the floor, he had nothing but thoughts of revenge on his mind. "Sod it, I'm going to get those kids and then they'll wish they'd never come here." Limping painfully, he crossed the main road to the red phone box, where he took four coins from his pocket, picked up the receiver of the black public phone and dialled the number displayed on Irina's business card. "Can I have a word with Miss Irina Slack please?"

"Speaking." The cold, polished female voice at the other end of line caused Sid to shiver. Irina Slack was not only Delano's second in command, she was also his most trusted companion.

"So, Mr. Planks, why don't you call round this afternoon at the address on the card – say about two? I think Dark Star may be able to offer you an interesting proposition."

"I'll be there bang on two. Thanks a lot Miss Slack, see you later. Bye now." Sid put the receiver down, feeling more than a little pleased with the invitation. It was beginning to look as though his big break had finally arrived. Grinning like a hyena, he limped off to fix up his aching ankle. There wouldn't be much decorating done today.

6 MEETINGS AND DEPARTURES

The warren of streets lined with old stone cottages twisted and turned from the river to the western edge of town. Midnight, silent and black as her name, zigzagged from one side of the road to the other as sections of pavement ran out on the left, and began again on the right. Toby and Daisy, walking at speed to keep up with their nimble guide, soon warmed up in the morning sunshine. Eventually, the houses thinned and the last street merged into a narrow lane where the presence of fields and trees alerted them to the fact that they had crossed the town boundary.

Shaded and partly hidden by conifers, a single storey dwelling built in honey stone came into view. The double gate had been left partly open affording them easy entry to a courtyard where a green vehicle was parked by the front door. The unusual design with wood panels on the outside had caught Toby's attention.

"It's a Morris Traveller," He fingered the unique wooden features, peering through the windows to check out the dashboard and seats. "Look at this Daise, historically it's so old but in Lumenor it's a brand new car. Wonder what it's like to ride in one of these?"

"I'm not interested in crappy old cars." Daisy, flounced over to the heavy oak door, where a grey slate sign announced that the house was called 'The Barn'. Breathing in the heady perfume of the purple wisteria flowers, which looked as if they were dripping down the wall, she began rapping the stag's head door- knocker.

Deep in concentration, Gabriel Greenway was decanting the last drop of lilac scented bath oil into a glass bottle whilst chanting some words in Ancient Lumen. Wiping his hands on a tea towel, he quickly removed his apron and went off to answer the door.

"Perfect timing," he announced, greeting the two new arrivals as the cat rubbed around his legs before slipping silently into the house. "Thanks Midnight, good job!"

"Hiya, you must be Gabriel then!" Daisy grabbed his hand and shook it heartily. "Morag sent us."

"I am," he replied," and you must be Daisy and Toby, the Lumerin have told me all about you," the twinkling brown eyes beamed at her. Gabriel's rich, deep voice and laid- back manner created an atmosphere of welcome and ease. "Follow me into my workshop. I just want to make sure everything's in order before we leave."

Shelves supporting a rainbow of glass bottles and jars lined the whitewashed walls of Gabriel's workshop where an array of drying bundles of flowers and herbs dangled from the beams. There were numerous pots and pans surrounding a solid green range, and on the wooden work tops to either side of the sink sat several silver bowls, a set of granite pestles and mortars, earthenware dishes, racks of test tubes and a Bunsen burner. On the chunky oak table in the centre, a half full jug of lilac oil waited to be poured into a neat row of pale green bottles.

"It smells totally lush in here." Daisy closed her eyes and inhaled deeply, "I wish we didn't have to leave so soon. My Grandma Evans says that some of the amazing things in life can be both sweet and bitter at the same time. When I think about finding and then leaving this gorgeous scented place, I understand what she meant."

Toby wandered around with interest examining the labels on

the jars and bottles. From time to time he would pause and turn his curiosity towards Gabriel. *Colouring's similar to mine, a touch darker, but I have straight hair … and he looks like a pirate*, he thought, taking in the deep bronze of the man's complexion, his loose black curls, the narrow gold knot-work bangle encircling his right wrist and the hoop earring in his left ear. Tall and lean in build, his new friend was casually dressed in black cords, soft checked shirt and a maroon waistcoat. *I feel like I've known him for years and that makes this new life in Lumenor much less scary than when we left Morag's.* Toby, now comfortable, enthusiastic and beginning to look forward to the journey, had totally ceased mourning the loss of his precious phone.

"I think the car's all packed." Gabriel strolled purposefully around his workshop checking that everything was arranged tidily and that all the surfaces were cleaned in readiness for his apprentice to take over.

"Joshua is learning to do general work with herbs flowers and plants as well as the more magical Lumerin things I'm teaching him about preparing potions. The Order needs to make sure that our secrets are passed on to the right people to keep the knowledge alive. At the moment, he's closing up the outbuilding. I never keep my lantern in the garden, because we're so close to the town. Last night I spoke with the Lumerin who have, of course, given precise instructions for the first leg of our journey."

"Certainly have." A cheerful eighteen-year-old in a red sweater breezed into the workshop, opened a cupboard, and placed a set of keys on a hook. "So this must be Toby and Daisy, the famous kids in that harp prophecy."

"Seems like it." Daisy couldn't help thinking how good the older boy looked in red.

"Hey, Sage!" he called. "It's really happening. Come and meet Toby and Daisy."

"Amazing," Sage Flowers answered on her way through the workshop door from the hall. "I'm Joshua's big sister … supplier of herbs and plants, a gardener. My work's supervised by the Lumerin so I plant according to their advice." Her long, cinnamon hair was pulled back into a ponytail, revealing a pretty oval face with olive complexion and clear hazel eyes that twinkled as much as Gabriel's. Daisy wished she had the time to visit Sage's garden. She wished there was time to talk to these new friends, but sadly, it was not to be.

"Look," said Gabriel addressing Sage and Joshua, "we have to get on the road pronto because there's already trouble. An odd job man, who sounds like that fool Sid Planks, attacked Daisy up by the Black Bull. It's certain that Irina Slack's been holding Dark Star recruitment meetings in the town hall and Planks is a regular there. He's been heard shouting his mouth off about joining. We have to suppose that he's already spoken to Irina and that, whatever Irina knows, Delano also knows."

"Morag says we've been sent here to find jewels for a special harp," Toby blurted out anxiously.

"That's true." Gabriel put a steadying hand on Toby's shoulder. "I know you're scared," he said, "If it's any consolation, I'm terrified too, it's just that I've mastered a few techniques that enable me to cope with being afraid. At the moment though, my lack of experience in caring for eleven year olds seems more frightening than Maxwell Delano. It's an entirely new thing for me you know, so you'll both need to exercise a great deal of patience. I've discovered the whereabouts of the first stone and we'll certainly be given information about the others whenever we need it."

"Are you sure about that?" Toby wasn't.

"Absolutely, the seven jewels have been placed in the keeping of some very reliable individuals in our Order with instructions to conceal them well. Delano will be in the north at Earthstill for the Eve of Threshold, so our task is to recover the stones and arrive there before the last day of the year. The Lumerin are sure that he'll have the means to corrupt the Heart of Stars by then, because he's very close now to finding the final words of the incantation he needs."

"Oh, that sounds well rubbish!" Daisy screwed her face up in disgust. "All that time in a car and it's probably going to get cold."

Toby, who really was doing his best to enjoy the adventure amidst his fear of the unknown and Maxwell Delano, had decided that it would at least be interesting to see more of Lumenor. "Yeah, but we might stay in some mega brilliant places and meet some fun people. You'll love that, Daisy," he insisted cheerfully.

Sociable, and always interested in a crowd, Daisy began to change her mind, though she admitted to being a wee bit worried about having only another two changes of (very dull) clothes.

"I suppose… so, it's a holiday, then," she sounded hesitant. "A sort of dangerous holiday, like some of those extreme sports."

The other four laughed as they made their way out to the courtyard.

"Remember," announced Sage, "a sense of humour provides one of the best shields ever against fear."

"I'll take your word for it." Daisy climbed into the car, opting for the back seat so that she could sit next to the small wicker basket containing several snacks for the journey including interesting packets of plain crisps containing little blue paper bags of salt.

"I'm in charge of food Toby, old pal, so you'd better try being extra nice to me or go hungry." Daisy's attempt at a wind up was doomed to failure.

"I'm too excited to care now, eat it all if you want," Toby clambered into the front passenger seat. "I've got the best view."

"I've stashed the three rucksacks, herbal supplies and some equipment in the space behind the back seat," said Josh, interrupting any possibility of an argument "You're all set to go."

"Don't forget to feed Midnight," Gabriel reminded him, giving out last minute instructions. "Make sure that the doors are always locked even when you're at home. Talk to the Lumerin, but always secure the lantern room after twilight. Make lotions and potions and meet the orders as usual. The lilac bath oil needs to be finished of course, and then if anybody asks, I've gone on an expedition to locate a rare medicinal plant that's supposed to cure arthritis. I'll call from public phone boxes and Order of Lumen houses whenever I can."

"No problem, Gabriel. I know exactly what I'm doing. Relax! Everything will run exactly as it always does, because you've been a good teacher and, besides, I have Sage here to keep a watchful eye on me and nag if I get it wrong. Oh, and remember, you were eleven once though you have to admit it was a very long time ago," Joshua teased.

Gabriel ignored the comment as he went to give Sage an affectionate goodbye hug. She was the most reliable person he knew outside his immediate family and he really trusted her. He was more than happy to leave the Barn and Josh in her safekeeping until his return.

"I know there's little point in wasting energy thinking about the Eve of Threshold at this early stage in the journey."

"No, I agree," said Sage, "you shouldn't, it's ages to Threshold and I'll miss you. By the way, I think Toby's pretty laid back but you might have your work cut out with Daisy."

"You could be right." At that moment, Gabriel was really feeling the burden of his appointed task but kept those thoughts to himself. *I'm only 28, I'm young and there are so many good things I would like to do and learn,* he thought wistfully. *Why me? Why does this have to be my destiny?*

Those questions only caused feelings of weakness and misery and he knew he had to snap out of it. *You have a job to do Greenway,* he told himself. *Time to face up to the reality of being born a guardian in the Order of Lumen.* Holding that idea, Gabriel jumped swiftly into the Morris Traveller and turned the key in the ignition.

"Okay," he said, fixing his attention on Daisy and Toby. "Let's go after that first stone."

Following Gabriel's departure, Josh quickly closed the gates and went indoors. He had made a decision to keep as busy as possible with the day-to-day running of business at The Barn in order to leave little time for feeling anxious. Gabriel Greenway, his great friend and mentor had been entrusted with the most awesome responsibility imaginable. "Destiny," he said, "who would have thought it would come to this?"

7 RED TOWER

Unaware of any departures, Sid Planks posed in front of the bathroom mirror, knotting his thin tie. He had forgotten to wash his best white shirt, so the collar looked slightly grubby around the edges, but, being Sid, he didn't think anybody would notice. The blue suit with narrow-cut trousers made him look pinched rather than elegant. After combing his hair with a popular greasy substance called Slickback, he went out to his battered grey van feeling very pleased with himself.

The imposing red brick house was perched on a hill twenty minutes north of Robinswood. The tower on the right hand side, and the fact that it was three floors high, made the building look very grand, as well as giving it the name 'Red Tower'.

From its elevated position, Red Tower's windows offered a good view of the road, so any unwelcome visitors would more than likely be noticed. Eyeing the high, pointed railings and matching gates, Sid understood how impossible it would be to get in without an appointment. After finding a convenient place to park, he walked up to the entrance and nervously pressed the buzzer. He jumped as the heavy gates swung inwards, allowing just enough time to step through before closing with a loud clang reminiscent of prison doors at lock-up.

"Blimey!" Sid gawped at the building from inside the railings. "More of a palace than a house. These people are obviously worth a bit. Can't be bad, eh?"

Before he had even reached the front door, it opened to reveal a plump, disagreeable woman with a sour face.

"Come in, then. You were expected at two o'clock and you're already five minutes late."

"Sorry, madam," replied Sid looking sheepish. "Traffic and all that."

Ignoring him, the moody housekeeper led the way in silence to a very elegant, pale grey room, furnished with squashy plum sofas and black velvet drapes.

Really fancy, thought Sid, afraid to say anything.

Irina Slack, dark haired and immaculately dressed in an expensive, tailored suit, put her glass down on the side table by the window, her manicured red nails clicking against the crystal as she did so.

"Ah, Mr. Planks," she said in that cold, polished voice. "Do sit down. Maxwell won't be a moment. Would you like a glass of wine?"

Sid, who didn't have any friends who drank wine, accepted with gratitude, his sallow cheeks reddening. His tie felt too tight and the woman's eyes seemed to bore right through him like lasers. He raised his glass to take a sip of his drink, hoping that it would help, but when he looked into its burgundy depths, he started to think of blood. He was relieved when Maxwell Delano finally entered the room.

Sid Planks had never seen anybody like Delano before and was not sure how to behave, so he remained silent, waiting until he was asked to speak. Maxwell Delano was one of those intimidating people you wouldn't be able to say no to and although he was only of average height, his presence seemed to fill the entire room. The groomed steely grey hair and pallid, unlined face served to emphasize a pair of eyes that were deep and scary, like black holes.

The man's face reminded Sid of a frozen landscape, though he had no idea why. Still, the smart dark suit, the carefully starched shirt, the gold tie clip and cufflinks gave the impression that Delano was obviously very wealthy and that he might be prepared to pay hefty wages for any job he needed doing.

"Mr. Planks." Delano's tone sounded so icy and stark, like the landscape in Sid's imagination.

He began to shiver a little, experiencing a sudden chill as Delano continued.

"I understand that you encountered two strange children by the Black Bull this morning."

"Yes, Sir." Planks sounded nervous. "Horrible kids, as well. Ran off down Lott's Lane in the direction of the bridge."

"Greenway!" hissed Delano, clenching his fist and screwing up his black hole eyes. "My guess is that they've already left."

"What?" exclaimed Sid, puzzled and shocked by the intensity of Delano's vicious manner.

"Gabriel Greenway, Mr. Planks, is one of the more important younger men in the Order of Lumen," replied Delano. "They've gone to look for the harp jewels. It seems the Order, have discovered a prophecy about these kids. They have to be stopped from finding those stones, and making their way to the north. Do you think that you can round up a couple more men and be ready to leave this evening? I don't care what you do with the kids - or Greenway for that matter - as long as you stop them and get the stones. You'll be paid so well, if you succeed, that you'll be set up for life."

It was just what Sid had hoped for. Not only time off, but a big payout. He knew of two good lads who would be happy to come with him for a lump of cash and some aggro.

"What do you mean about the stones? And what's this Order of Lumen?" he asked, as Delano took few steps towards the door.

"Irina will fill you in on the details." Maxwell Delano was already bored with his guest. "My own man, Hugo Shade, will be going with you in the vehicle I have provided and you will do exactly what he tells you, without question. He'll be at the Black Bull ready to leave promptly at seven. Make sure that you're on time. Welcome to Dark Star."

"Thanks a million Mr. Delano" Sid extracted himself from the plummy folds of the sofa. He was so excited that he could hardly keep still. " You can count on me, I won't let you down."

"Make sure you don't, Mr. Planks." Maxwell moved closer to Sid, fixing him with a hypnotic stare that stabbed like a knife. "It really is important not to let me down. Ever!"

Delano left the room without a single backward glance.

Shivering again with fright and cold, Sid backed away, but soon recovered, warming up to a comfortable temperature as soon as he remembered the enormous pay packet he'd been promised.

* * * *

Following an interesting talk with Irina Slack, Sid Planks made his way home. He really didn't have a clue that all this stuff had been going on in Lumenor, but now he did know, he definitely wanted to be in on it. Maxwell Delano wasn't someone you could mess with and Sid had a lot of respect for that. This Order of Lumen didn't seem to have much going for them in comparison, especially that Gabriel Greenway, who seemed to be some sort of soppy soap maker. The lads would soon sort him out if he made any fuss.

Sid called round to see his two best mates, Barry Mackintosh and Jack Scally, who lived in the same street. He was certain to find them at home because they only worked on their market stall in the mornings. The three of them had all been at school together, where they had wasted most of their time trying to be as much of a nuisance as possible.

In contrast to Sid, Barry was stocky with broad shoulders and hands like shovels. Always grinning and making a noise, he was prone to hitting people first and asking questions later. Jack, however - lean and athletic - never had much to say for himself. He didn't often waste energy on mindless aggression, but when Jack needed to get even, he planned it carefully for maximum effect. This tendency made him a much more dangerous prospect than the other two.

Once they had gathered at Barry's place it didn't take Sid very long to persuade his friends to go along with his plans, as they were also becoming Dark Star supporters and attending some of the local meetings. Neither Jack nor Barry had heard of the Order of Lumen because sadly, like Sid, their parents had never told them stories, and they had never cared for reading books themselves.

"See you at The Bull at seven, then, lads. We have to meet some bloke called Hugo Shade. Apparently, Maxwell Delano has hired him to do all the planning for the trip, and our instructions are to do what we are told without question. Pack a bag as quick as you can. Oh, and we'll be going in his car, which I suspect will be a big flashy one, so try to look just a bit smart."

"Sounds ace," said Jack. "My cousin Eric's out of work so I'll arrange for him to cover the stall and then we're all set. See you later."

Grinning all over his vacant face, Barry shut the door after Sid and Jack then went upstairs to sort out a bag of clothes. I hope that there's gonna be some fisticuffs and fun while we're earning this money, he thought, in any case, it 'll make a nice change from the usual daily grind of selling dodgy kitchenware.

* * * *

Hugo Shade, thirty years old, chocolate skinned and sharp suited, considered himself to be an ultra stylish and important individual. The elegant, silver-grey mac draped around his shoulders, the matching felt hat and whiff of expensive cologne completed the carefully planned effect. He was one of those pushy superior types who always take over even when they're wrong, then make people with less confidence feel as small as possible.

It wasn't long before Maxwell Delano himself had spotted Hugo and taken him under his wing, sensing that the ruthless ambition would prove very useful within Dark Star's Inner

Circle. Though Shade would step on anybody to get his own way, he remained in awe of Maxwell Delano, a man with a power over people that Hugo himself had not yet been able to acquire. Max, his hero as well as his teacher, had given Hugo some special information, which had to remain a secret between the two of them until the time was right. Not even Irina would know.

"It will be our secret," Max had said. "Tell nobody... not even other important people in Dark Star." Hugo was well pleased with his good fortune and in addition to Max's trust he had been given the latest brand new black Jaguar car for his personal use. It all went so perfectly with his wonderful opinion of himself.

At ten to seven, Hugo and the car in question were waiting outside the Black Bull for the three men he knew Delano had hired for him. Hugo, who thoroughly enjoyed a chase, relished the idea of trashing the Order of Lumen's plans and stealing their precious harp jewels. He felt like he had been born just for this. "It 's so ME," he said, voicing his opinion out loud.

He thought of Red Tower and the ceremony that Maxwell and Irina would begin at seven, to call the Dark Star into the tarnished silver lantern. He became energized as he pictured that coal black glittering stream of energy, curving like a serpent into a corrupted crystal, long ago turned muddy and murky from its encounters with this black light. Dark Star ruled his world and he loved it.

"Hugo Shade?" inquired a voice behind him.

Hugo turned round to see three scruffy, tough looking men gazing with admiration at his new car. "That's me," he sneered.

"Sid Planks, Jack Scally and Barry Mackintosh," said Sid by way of introduction. "We've been hired by Maxwell Delano."

Hugo's response wasn't exactly friendly, which made Jack Scally think *he's not a barrel of laughs is he? The creep gave me a look like he'd just stepped in something nasty.* Jack had taken an instant dislike to Hugo, though he was trying hard not to let it show. He intended to wait and see how things panned out during the

43

trip. Gifted with a better than average ability to sense Jack's hostility, Hugo Shade smirked and ignored it. After all, he didn't get where he was today by being Mr. Popular, and Scally was just a very small pawn in a very big game.

"Greenway's car was seen heading south at around half twelve," he explained, switching attention to his appointed task, "so that's the direction we must take. Max has a good idea where they're going. Get in the Jag, there's room in the boot for your bags."

Relaxed and aggressively smooth like a prowling panther, Shade turned on the engine, his mouth twisting into a nasty smile as the car purred away from the Black Bull. He was really going to enjoy this job and couldn't wait to get Greenway and those meddling kids. It would be sweet thinking up mental tortures and other foul ways to make their lives miserable.

Hugo was so smug, *It's apparent,* he thought to himself, *the three monkeys I've been given won't cause me any problems. People like that are always easy to manipulate; they just follow the crowd if they think they can get something out of it, and if for any reason they fail to shape up, then they're definitely very expendable.*

8 THE FIRST STONE

Long before Hugo Shade left Robinswood, the meddling kids and Gabriel Greenway had already covered a good distance, travelling first south and then west along country roads in the hope of avoiding recognition. Toby remarked that he had never seen so many sheep and cows in the whole of his life, or, for that matter, so much grass and woodland. It was as though the whole world had turned green, pushing concrete, traffic jams and shopping centres into distant memory. Every now and then, they passed through a hamlet or village without stopping, as Gabriel preferred to stay away from people.

"We have to be careful. I don't know exactly how far-reaching the Dark Star organization has become, but I suspect that it might have spread out into some of our villages. There could be spies anywhere."

"I don't know anything about Dark Star," said Toby, " so far, we've only met Sid Planks. He's a moron, a slimy skanky rat."

"Granted," agreed Gabriel, "but he's a dangerous rat and it would be unwise to underestimate him."

"Have you ever met Maxwell Delano then Gabriel?" Daisy's sudden need to know overcame her fear.

"When I was a boy, I met him once with my parents on Ynys yr Delyn before he changed allegiance and began seeking dark knowledge. My father said Max was a bit of a loner, never really fitting in, and getting angry if he thought people were slighting him. Stupid really, because the Order of Lumen doesn't go in for gossip and intrigue, so nobody would have had any interest in putting him down. It was all in his head. He always wanted to be in charge, to have control, while the rest of us co-operated, acknowledging each person's qualities and purpose in the world. Delano went his own way until he became cut off from the Order and, even worse, from the Lumerin. Some of the Elders did try to help but he would have none of it."

"So, nasty Max started all this to become more important than everybody else right," summarized Toby. " That's well pathetic!"

"I guess so," continued Gabriel. "The sad thing is that he was once an excellent musician and scholar of Ancient Lumen. It was from texts in the old language, long hidden to prevent misuse, that he found references to the Dark Star Chronicles and the Isle of Storms. He's been learning chants and can call the Dark Star beings in the same way as we call the Lumerin. He hasn't yet found the words to corrupt the Heart of Stars and change its song - but if he does, the creative, gentle lives we all enjoy will be changed forever."

It was a depressing prospect which caused both Toby and Daisy to stop looking at the scenery and fall back into their own private thoughts for the last few miles of the journey.

"Look, there's my old pal Dion!" Gabriel slowed the car and came to a halt alongside a gleaming, powerful motorbike. Daisy roused herself to see what was happening. A striking looking man with shoulder length, nut- brown hair and piercing green eyes was suddenly greeting Gabriel through the open driver's window. She wrinkled her nose at the pungent smell of white hawthorn blossoms wafting from the hedgerow.

"Can't tell you how glad we are to see you," said Gabriel

"Follow me!" The stranger took the lead. "I sensed your approach about half an hour ago, so I decided to come and meet you myself. We can park up at the house and go straight out to find what you've come for, then we'll be able to relax for a few days and make plans."

Revving up his bike again, Dion Hawke rode away, with Gabriel putting his foot down to keep up. Ten minutes later, they were all piling out of the car in front of a substantial Victorian house surrounded by the magnificent trees that had given it the name 'Oaklands'. Because there were no other dwellings in sight, the isolation afforded Toby and Daisy a renewed sense of safety.

Dion Hawke's striking resemblance to a bird of prey made Daisy wonder just how far he might actually be able to see. She hadn't forgotten that this Hawke man had sensed them half an hour away. How is it possible for anyone to do that? She was a little shy of him, thinking how glad she was that he was a friend and not an enemy.

Olivia Hawke emerged from the house, waving her arms in greeting as she ran down the steps from the front door. Whilst Morag had reminded Toby of the moon, he likened Olivia to the Earth at harvest time, with her wild, copper curls, emerald eyes and golden complexion. He liked her immediately, because she had abundant warmth, which made him feel very welcome.

"I hope you're not too tired to walk after your journey, it's not far."

"No," lied Toby, secretly wanting to put his feet up and eat something, but also eager for the adventure. It seemed like ages since they had left Morag and Finn, but it was, in fact, now close to four in the afternoon. About the same amount of time had passed as a day in school, but packed with such different experiences that there hadn't been much time to think.

"I for one will be glad of the opportunity to stretch my legs after that drive," added Gabriel as they followed Dion around the back of the house, over a stile and across a paddock to the edge of a pinewood. This time, there was no gate across the pathway leading into the trees and after a short walk, he turned off the path to the left, leading them through clumps of new ferns to a log cabin in a small clearing.

"This is where we come to call the Lumerin. Our lantern's in the cabin and, as this land belongs to Oaklands, other people rarely come here without an invitation."

"It's not twilight,' Daisy was puzzled, "Morag said you always call the Lumerin at twilight."

"Dion and I will return later to call the Lumerin," Olivia explained, "but right now we have another task, which is best carried out in daylight. Come, let's continue on into the wood."

Returning to the path and heading further into the trees, Dion finally called a halt under the branches of a very tall spruce.

"Quiet," he ordered. "I need to concentrate."

He began a sharp whistle, which cut the air like a sword. Toby and Daisy were on tenterhooks, wondering what on Earth was going to happen next, when the sound of flapping wings brought them a kestrel. The bird circled around a couple of times before settling comfortably on Dion's wrist. Toby recognized a happy greeting, not so much in words, but in the feeling of pleasure you get from meeting a friend you haven't seen for ages.

They all listened as Dion spoke to the bird in a language that the two young ones had come to recognize as Ancient Lumen. They still had little idea what was being said, but the sound was already familiar and Toby was actually beginning to pick up individual words.

Soaring high into the upper branches of the spruce, the kestrel found a small hole in the trunk, which from the ground could only be seen by someone with exceptional vision. A minute later, the bird returned to deposit a worn leather pouch into Dion's out-stretched palm.

"Thank-you, Rory," he said in Ancient Lumen as the bird moved around on his wrist, before unfolding his wings and taking off into the treetops with a shrill, goodbye squawk.

"Great hiding place," said Gabriel. "Only you could think of that, Dion."

"We do what we're able. Now, let's see what Rory has brought for us."

A brilliant, many faceted, jewel, as blue as cornflowers and about an inch and a half in diameter, fell into his palm as he tipped up the pouch.

"Are we peaceful and inspired?" he asked. "This is the Stone of Peace and Inspiration, ready to be returned to its rightful place."

Daisy and Toby had never seen anything so beautiful. The jewel's luminous blue depths and expertly cut facets gave it a light and energy all of its own, creating an impression of a living being rather than a stone. Looking into it made them think of rainbows, sweet music and stunning, unearthly landscapes. They were so enthralled it was difficult to look away, until Dion replaced the gem in its pouch and handed it to Daisy.

"You can't seriously want me to look after this. I mean everyone knows that I'm rubbish at responsibility. Ask Toby!" Daisy began to show signs of panic. "What if I lose it?"

"Have a little more faith in yourself, Daisy." Olivia had already thought out the arrangements. "I have three leather belts with a bag threaded onto each one so that you and Toby can each carry two stones, and Gabriel can carry three. The responsibility is then shared, and the gems will never all be in the same location, just in case one of you is caught. Don't forget, the stones are effective as a set."

"Nobody's getting caught," interrupted Gabriel. "Come on, Daisy, put it in your pocket until we get back to the house."

Rallying a little, Daisy did as she was told and, twenty minutes later, they were indoors, looking forward to a meal and a rest. Toby examined the beautiful carvings of birds placed carefully on individual tables in the hall, seeing which ones he could recognize.

Seated at last in the lounge, the creator of the art was revealed. "I'm a woodcarver," Dion explained. "My work sells all over Lumenor because the figures have Soul, but, of course, nobody really knows just how much I can understand and blend with the birds I carve. Olivia's a well-known storyteller and poet. Her communication with the Lumerin is a mystery and her work contains their light. This is how we make our living in the world."

Toby turned his attention on Gabriel. "And what about you?"

"Let me see," the reply was modest. "I have a reputation in the Order of Lumen for building a positive attitude and curing illness and injury with my lotions and potions. When I chant over them, I call the life-giving light of the Lumerin into the liquids. My everyday customers, who obviously don't know this, get much more than they paid for. As well as a quality product, there's a better feeling in the mind, so to speak. Like Sage, I have a very close relationship with plants, much the same as Dion has with birds. The Lumerin do the rest, because I co-operate with them. On the whole, I don't worry much because life always works out for the best if I follow their instructions. I don't feel separate from either the world or the universe I exist in, and that's how I can understand both the plants and the Lumerin. Somehow that connection has pulled you and Daisy into Lumenor at exactly the right time. It's magic and it's amazing. "

"Brilliant or what!' Toby began to laugh as the penny dropped regarding the Order of Lumen. "Unlike Delano and Planks, you all use your talents to help because you respect each other and the world you inhabit, so then things seem to fall into place and it's fun."

"Got it," approved Olivia, who, on that positive note, went out to fetch the food. Dion got up to help, leaving the other three friends to relax.

"I expect we'll have to leave tomorrow," moaned Daisy, looking sadly at Gabriel. "We never have time for anything." She checked the leather pouch in her pocket to make sure it was still there.

Gabriel glanced kindly at her. "No, Daisy, this time, you don't have to leave immediately. We're going to stay a while. The Lumerin have already decided on a course of action. Dion and Olivia will be talking to them again after our meal to get more precise information but right now I'm famished and I can smell roast chicken. Dion and Olivia are great cooks. Let's eat!"

"That's tidy then." Daisy, pleased to be staying, had begun to chill out as their hosts arrived with the serving dishes. The feast on the dining table was most welcome after the first stressful day journeying into the unknown. The starter of fresh warm bread rolls and their hosts' homemade leek and potato soup was very tasty.

"Well," said Toby, taking a second chunk of bread to mop up the last of his soup, "at this precise moment, here we are with loyal friends, warm food, and I'm happy, so what could possibly go wrong?"

9 FISH AND CHIPS

After two whole hours on the road, Barry Mackintosh was feeling decidedly peckish because he hadn't eaten since the corned beef and brown sauce sandwiches he'd made and devoured around five-thirty. The novelty of the new Jaguar had soon worn off, turning Barry's instincts back towards his usual pursuits. He was beginning to wish he could be with some of the lads in the Black Bull for a pint of beer, a packet of crisps and the promise of fish and chips on the way home.

"I'm starving! How about stopping at a chip shop?"

"Good idea, Barry," agreed Jack. "That'd fill us up for the rest of the night."

Gripping the steering wheel just a little tighter, Hugo Shade's face twisted into an expression of distaste.

"I've no intention of stopping anywhere and if you think you're going to be eating greasy food in my new car then you're sadly mistaken. You can just wait until we get to Swallowdale."

"How long's that going to be?" Barry became petulant.

"About another two hours." Hugo was really enjoying the torture. "Give or take a bit, of course."

"The chip shops'll all be closed," whined Sid, feeling disappointed.

Hugo sneered. "Too bad." He hadn't the slightest grain of sympathy. "Perhaps if you're lucky, our hosts, the Batts, will have a snack for you when we arrive."

There was no point in arguing. Shade was as rigid as a brick wall. Having said what he wanted to say, he created an atmosphere of unfriendly silence between himself and his passengers. He had a sense that the two in the rear seat were sticking imaginary knives in his back, but wasn't worried in the least. In fact, he was rather pleased with himself for causing this tasty bit of torment. Eventually, the disgruntled passengers fell asleep, leaving him to his own dark thoughts.

At roughly eleven o'clock, the Jaguar entered the main street in the village of Swallowdale. Taking a sharp left into a lane, Shade stopped in front of a small cottage with a paddock. The lack of motion and engine noise woke the passengers.

"Great!" exclaimed Sid in total relief. "We must be here!" The other two rubbed their eyes, taking a couple of minutes to adjust before venturing out into the chilly starlit night.

Hugo Shade sniffed the country air with disgust. There was a definite whiff of pigs, which clashed unpleasantly with his favourite must have designer cologne. He dumped the bags impatiently on the roadside before retrieving his own suitcase on wheels and his black leather briefcase from the boot.

"So, here we are," he observed snootily. "Irina has made the arrangements, and we're expected. Doesn't look much, does it?"

Jack Scally was in just the right mood for an argument. "All we want is a bit of nosh, maybe a beer and somewhere to kip for the night. We're not so bothered about your fancy stuff."

"Easily pleased, then," replied Hugo sarcastically, banging on the door with considerable force.

Malina Batt's thin face appeared in the open doorway. Shade summed her up quickly - about sixty, unhealthy, greasy hair and creased blouse, messy wretch. He hoped that the kitchen would at least be clean as he rudely pushed past her, with only a curt greeting. As the other three men followed him, an equally messy Douglas Batt, emerged from the untidy living room to greet his guests.

"As you can see, Mr. Shade," he said, addressing Hugo, "we

haven't much space here, so I hope you'll be all right up in the attic. It's just one long room with four mattresses. The family use it when they stay."

Shade winced at the thought of a communal dormitory, but, nevertheless, followed Doug upstairs, promising himself he would sort it out tomorrow with a quick phone call to Irina Slack. *Gross*, thought Hugo, *there must be a decent hotel with an en-suite bathroom around here, or a better Dark Star house more in keeping with my position.*

There was only one bathroom on the first floor and the once-white bath had a scummy ring around the inside. The second bedroom was full of junk.

In the attic, the four visitors put their bags by their individual mattresses. Hugo claimed the one under the window in case he had need of fresh air, but when he remembered the awful pig smell, he thought twice about opening it.

"Nosh is on the table," Malina screeched up the stairwell. "Doug went out for fish and chips just before the shop shut. I've been keeping them warm in the oven for you. We've got some beer as well."

"Thanks a ton… I'm starving," grinned Barry, licking his lips in anticipation. "See," he taunted Hugo, "we got our chips after all."

There was no reply, only another brick wall.

Around the kitchen table, the Batts and three of their guests decided to finish up the night with a friendly game of cards and Shade felt relieved to get some space from people he considered to be his inferiors. Hugo had eaten less than half the food on his plate.

"I'm turning in now," he announced haughtily, handing Douglas enough money to pay for supper. "Here, the meal's on Maxwell Delano." The tone was condescending, designed to make Doug think that he was being given a handout.

With the comfort of a full stomach, Sid had forgotten about Shade's closeness to Delano and his position in Dark Star.

"We'll try not to make a noise when we turn in," he said,

attempting to sound as though he cared.

"I don't like him much," complained Jack as soon as Hugo had gone to bed. "Gives me the creeps."

"And me," agreed Sid, "but compared to his boss, I'm sure he's a pussycat and we're going to make a packet. It's only a job and it'll set us up for life, remember? Best not cause any trouble, eh Jack? Shade's very high up in Dark Star, and Delano has put him in charge."

Sid Planks was experiencing a vivid memory of his encounter with Maxwell Delano at Red Tower. Feeling an unexpected chill, he shivered, recalling Max's cruel expression, pallid complexion, eyes like black holes and words about not messing up. Sid had no intention of letting Max down, so he would be having another little talk with Jack when they had a minute alone. Right now, though, his sprained ankle was aching from sitting in a car for hours. A game of cards, with a beer by the fire, was just what he wanted.

Hugo, on the other hand, was congratulating himself on being Dark Star elite, a member of Max Delano's privileged inner circle. The less important people were downstairs amusing themselves with their simple pursuits.

Some of us are just born to rule, he thought lying down on the uncomfortable mattress in his new silk pyjamas and pulling up the rough blankets. Hugo didn't do relationships unless there was something big in it for him.

Even so, he passed a disturbed night listening to the others snoring until the harsh sound of a crowing cockerel at dawn was the last straw. After attempting a minimal wash in the dubious bathroom, he left the house in search of fresh air. He had forgotten about the pigs until the sickening stench of manure on his empty stomach propelled him back inside. There was no one else up yet, so he made an early morning phone call to Irina Slack.

"Listen, Irina, it's a bit cramped here. Isn't there another Dark Star house in the area? I could do with more space to think clearly."

"There's no other Dark Star house in that area Hugo but there's a rather good hotel on the main road in Half Moon Cross about ten minutes away… so why don't you leave the others at Doug's and book yourself a room there? Max said to tell you to charge any expenses you need to him. However, be sure to check in with Planks every day, I don't want those three fools wandering around without supervision in case they cause trouble and draw attention to us."

"Thanks, Irina." Hugo breathed a sigh of relief. The expense account confirmed his privileged position.

Irina continued. "I believe that there are some important Order of Lumen members somewhere within a thirty mile radius of Swallowdale and Greenway might well be with them. As yet, we've no idea of their exact position or even who they are. You'll have to do some snooping around."

"Will do," replied Hugo.

"Oh, and Hugo," Irina reminded him. "We're counting on you, and Max doesn't like failure."

"Of course not," Shade replied without the slightest hint of worry.

"Instruct Planks and his friends to start searching around Swallowdale. They need to find out if anyone's seen Greenway and those two kids, or even just Greenway's car. I know there are a lot of Morris Travellers in the countryside, but it's a start. People notice everything in small places."

Sid, Barry and Jack finally surfaced around nine-thirty after an uninterrupted heavy sleep. Oblivious to the ring around the bath and the junk in the second bedroom, they were very pleased with their lodgings, especially when the aroma of frying bacon filled their nostrils as they came downstairs.

"Ten minutes to breakfast!" Malina banged loudly on a frying pan. "Bacon from our own little porkers."

Following Hugo out to the Jag, they listened carefully to his orders as the two items of luggage went back into the boot. Sid was especially happy at the separation as it meant that Jack would have less chance to get wound up.

Shade handed Sid a piece of paper with the address and phone number of the Half Moon Hotel. "I'll be back tomorrow, so make sure you've spent your time looking and not just messing about. Max is expecting results."

Jack was thinking, *Good riddance,* as he eyed Hugo with a closed expression. He had decided to be good to Sid and toe the line at least for now.

Shade delivered one last withering look before driving away in search of his comfortable hotel, where he hoped to find privacy, good food, no pigs and most important, a spotlessly clean en-suite bathroom.

10 AN UNPLEASANT ENCOUNTER

Toby, Daisy and Gabriel relaxed in an atmosphere of warmth and new pursuits, as time at Oaklands passed in a burst of bright blossoms and bold fresh greens.

Toby took long walks with Dion, discovering all he could about birds and animals, as well as becoming very successful at communicating with them. He had no idea how he could know what they were saying to him, but he was quickly learning to accept his gift and to stop questioning whether or not it was real. After getting to know Dion's birds, he had made friends with several squirrels, a couple of foxes and some deer.

"I'm really impressed with your progress," Dion told him, "you pay attention and learn quickly,"

"I'm enjoying every minute and for the first time I can really be myself instead of what other people expect me to be."

Meanwhile, Gabriel, who had been locating the positions of various appropriate plants and herbs, had set up a tiny, temporary laboratory in the corner of the kitchen to brew a few potions especially for the journey.

"A good herbalist," he insisted, "never travels anywhere without a small box of equipment. The Lumerin have taught me how to make special products which are not meant for the normal market - potions to help us get through the chilly depths of Earthstill and any other difficult situations we may encounter before the year is over. These new recipes contain more magic than chemistry. It's a real challenge."

Daisy, for her part, had never had so much fun. After Olivia presented her with a large box of paints, some brushes and thick paper, she began to create pictures taking inspiration from the colour inside her. There were birds, animals and plants whose forms were all exploding with vibrant tones and appeared so alive that it would make you happy just to look at them. Then, she began to design unusual garments, describing them as clothes to feel good in.

"I wish we had the time together to cut and sew some of these clothes," said Daisy who had become quite attached to Olivia.

"I'd like that too," replied Olivia, breathing deeply to prevent a wave of sadness from overwhelming her. She knew all too well that she and Daisy would soon be separated, most likely forever, whatever the outcome for Lumenor.

After much deliberation and conversation with the Lumerin, they all decided that the best time for departure from Oaklands would be on the first day of Greening. On this, the longest day of the year, the power of light would be very strong, affording them extra protection and good energy from the sun.

As the final few days of Floria had brought warmer weather, Olivia took the cousins to the small market town of Mayberry, some ten miles away, to purchase shorts, extra summer tops for the sunny days ahead, and sensible leather sandals for walking. They would be leaving the day after tomorrow, so the mission had become urgent. Daisy gratefully accepted the new footwear, without trying to persuade Olivia to buy the dazzling gold party sandals she preferred rather than the practical, brown leather ones she needed.

She had settled down since she had been painting, designing and walking out in the fields and woods with Toby. Her confidence and independence had substantially increased, making her posture straighter and stilling any need for rebellion or seeking attention and approval.

She loved to watch the animals and birds come when Toby called or whistled. Sometimes, they would arrive as if in response to his thoughts. Toby, in turn, was knocked out by Daisy's paintings of the creatures he had grown to love. A deep respect was developing between them.

The time at Oaklands had been like the most wonderful holiday, but unfortunately, like most holidays, it was destined to come to an end. Leaving the shoe shop first, Toby had a shock. Pushing Daisy back into the doorway, he made a hasty retreat after her. He could scarcely believe it. On the other side of the road, outside a newsagent's shop, was the familiar, slimy figure of Sid Planks in conversation with two equally unpleasant men.

Olivia, leaving the counter after making her purchases, registered the alarm on Toby's face as he ducked into the shop.

"Oh pants, I don't believe it!" His eyes were wide with dismay. "It's Sid Planks! He's outside!"

"Are you sure?" Olivia, who had never actually met Sid Planks, went to the doorway to take a look, "stay out of sight, both of you."

Daisy just managed to sneak a quick peek, recognizing her former attacker immediately. There was an unpleasant memory, the sour taste of his bony hand in her mouth from the morning in Robinswood, when she had bitten him and Toby had followed up her bravery with that well-aimed kick.

"Stay behind me," instructed Olivia, guiding Toby and Daisy into a corner away from the door. "We must be patient and wait until they move away."

"I do hope Sid Planks isn't shopping for new shoes today," Daisy whispered taking a couple of deep breaths to calm her nerves. "I believe those three men are searching for us and that we are about to become fugitives." She clutched Toby's hand tightly for support.

As luck would have it, Sid, Barry and Jack were heading for the nearest pub with a good hour to kill before Hugo Shade picked them up for yet another boring drive around the neighbourhood. Apparently, Shade had received some promising information he was now checking out. With the usual preference for his own company, he had left the men in Mayberry to ask a few more questions and find somewhere to eat. They were now on their way to lunch, saying how great it was to get time off from horrible Hugo.

It was with an enormous sense of relief that Olivia watched them walk away up the street and out of sight.

"They've gone! Quick, we must vanish!" she urged, pushing Toby and Daisy outside in the opposite direction to the one that Planks and the others had taken. Hurrying down a side street, they reached the car park by a more obscure route, piling into Olivia's pale blue Morris 1000 to head off towards the open countryside.

Lunch was the last thing on Olivia's mind as they made the return journey, using the lesser known lanes. She needed to be with Dion so that they could discuss what to do. So much depended on these two youngsters she had grown to care for and there could be no mistakes now. It was such a relief to reach the gates of Oaklands and the safety of her own home.

"Am I pleased to see you," Dion, tense from sensing Olivia's alarm for more than half an hour was pacing about in the lounge. Gabriel had also stopped his potion brewing in order to join his friend. There was strength in numbers.

"Oh, Gabriel!" cried Daisy. " It's really bad. Sid Planks was in town with two other nasty looking men. We saw them just as we were leaving the shoe shop."

Gabriel's shoulders slumped a little at the bad news.

"That's not what I wanted to hear, is there any way you could have been mistaken?" he asked, already knowing what the response would be.

Toby hook his head. "I really wish that we could tell you it's mistake, but we can't." He looked at Gabriel for help.

"You must go tomorrow," Dion decided. "I know it's only the Eve of Greening, but you'll soon enter the dawn of the longest day and I'm sure the protection will be almost as good."

"It makes sense," Gabriel agreed. "We'll pack now, then load the car up tonight ready for an early departure in the morning."

After packing their rucksacks, Toby and Daisy went out for one last walk, promising to stay close to the house and not to go beyond the wood. As soon as they left, Dion whistled for Rory, "Keep an eye on my young friends and return immediately if you spot any strangers in either the wood or the field around it. Should anything untoward happen and you can't get back in time, call in help from the kites and ravens" Rory flew off, happy to be useful.

11 AIR FORCE

Sitting by the lantern house, Daisy pulled the Stone of Peace and Inspiration from the leather bag on her belt and held it up to catch the light from a bright sunbeam, which had strayed through a gap between the pines.

"Gabriel says the next stone's for protection," she informed Toby. "I expect you or him might have to look after that one. Although Gabriel knows who's been entrusted with its safety, we have to follow instructions the Lumerin will provide for us today because the next destination is supposed to be a little trickier."

Toby hadn't thought much about stones until that close encounter with Sid Planks had forced him to remember the reason he was in Lumenor in the first place. Still, some protection might come in useful. It was so much like the day before the end of a holiday that it brought on thoughts of home.

"I hope our parents are alright." His voice shook as he voiced his fears. "I'm worried about them. We have been away so long that they've got to be frantic by now."

Daisy agreed, placing her hands on Toby's shoulders and watching the delicate greens and yellows streaming from her fingers. "Just now, I really miss them right, though I have to say, I don't miss school. We've no choice, so I suppose we'll just have to get on with this and, maybe, if it all works out, we'll see them again."

Toby clambered to his feet newly energized from Daisy's colours and a successful attempt to heed Gabriel's advice about trying to stay in the present. It was never an easy thing to do. "I hope so. Come on, Daise, let's go talk to some squirrels and a few birds before we go back to the house."

"Great." Daisy sighed as she made an effort to find enough enthusiasm to follow him into the trees.

Thanks to the squirrels and a couple of friendly jays, they left the wood in a more upbeat mood an hour later, unaware that an unwelcome visitor had called at Oaklands in their absence. Dion appeared agitated as the two young people entered the lounge. It was completely out of character - Dion was usually so cool.

"Thank goodness you went out. We've had a visitor, a man called Hugo Shade. He was sneaking around in front of the house, and when I confronted him, he claimed to be looking for a couple of children who are supposed to be missing. There was something about him that made me think of a black bottomless pit. My instincts tell me that he's most certainly high ranking Dark Star, and as you've already seen Sid Planks, I can only assume the two are connected."

"I know about Hugo Shade and in fact, I've even seen him in Robinswood," Gabriel added, "I'm pretty sure he has a top position in Dark Star, and that he's one of Maxwell Delano's favourites. The word is that he's both cruel and ruthless - someone who'd stop at nothing to get what he wants."

Toby cowered at the mention of Delano; the unwelcome addition of this Hugo Shade had created a new threat. The fun was well and truly over. "What are we going to do?" he asked, his voice shaking a little from that nameless fear creeping back into him.

"Firstly," affirmed Olivia, putting a protective arm around Toby, "I think we should have our meal and then, later, Gabriel and I will go to the wood for a conversation with the Lumerin. You and Daisy can stay here with Dion and keep out of sight.

We'll pack the car after dark. Shade definitely hasn't seen it because it's still locked in one of the garages."

Toby regained his composure. His friends were so positive that it was difficult to remain in a state of anxiety for long. The evening passed without any further disruption so Toby and Daisy turned in soon after Gabriel and Olivia returned from the lantern house, both falling into a deep sleep until sunrise.

Arriving in the kitchen, they were surprised to find Olivia and Dion up and about. Dion had already been out, at dawn, talking to friends, as he put it. What he really meant was that he had been alerting his birds of prey to summon maximum backup just in case.

It really was time to go. Daisy, as usual, was sad and even Toby, who was trying to be brave, had difficulty holding back a tear or two. They had just finished their parting hugs when the black Jaguar arrived. "Go now, there's no more time!" Dion was pushing them hastily towards the back door in the kitchen, then in a flash, they were in the rear courtyard, running for the security of their car.

Risking his own safety, in the firm intention of stalling Dark Star, Dion was confronted by a snarling Hugo Shade and three rough men as he opened the front door. Outnumbered, he put up a strong fight, but was unable to break away. Dragged along the hallway by Sid and his thugs, he was pushed into the front room and held captive. Olivia screamed when Hugo Shade stormed in after them, grabbing hold of her copper curls and wrapping his long arm tightly around her neck. The others soon followed, keeping a firm hold on the struggling Dion, who made as much fuss as possible to keep Shade's attention away from Gabriel and the Morris Traveller.

"Leave her alone scum!" Dion growled, his eyes blazing as he continued his attempts to break free from Jack and Barry who between them held their captive in a powerful unrelenting grip.

"Not until you give me those kids!" commanded Shade, unmoved and confident.

"I don't know what kids you're talking about," Dion

confronted him, poker faced.

Both men locked eyes in a battle of wills as the order to give up the children was repeated. At the same time, Sid Planks was staring through the tall window in total disbelief. He couldn't for the life of him understand why there were so many birds perched in the oak trees and on the fence, and why hundreds more were still arriving. There were hawks, kestrels, kites, ravens, magpies, pigeons, and several other species that Sid didn't even recognize. Whatever was going on, he didn't much like it. Scally's jaw dropped with surprise and his grip on Dion loosened. The scene outside was completely unreal.

"Where did all those crazy birds come from?" he stammered with a puzzled frown.

"What birds?" barked Shade impatiently, forcing Olivia towards the window.

As he looked on in disbelief, the green Morris Traveller shot across the space in front of the house in the direction of the long, tree-lined drive, heading for the main road.

"It's Greenway!" Barry was beside himself, pointing his podgy finger at the window as he carelessly let go of Dion.

Hugo Shade was so angry that he almost burst into flames. Throwing Olivia away from him with so much force that she hit the wall, he ran to the front door like a wildcat, no longer interested in the hostages.

"Get a move on, morons!" he screeched at the three men, who shoved Dion aside in a mad dash to reach the exit.

"Get in the car!" Shade ordered, oblivious to the multitude of flapping birds even though the din was deafening.

Leaping into action, Dion followed them to the open doorway, and gave three loud, shrill whistles. From then on, the world of Dark Star became chaotic as feathered predators hurled themselves from the trees, first at Hugo and then at the other three, pulling their hair and ripping their clothes with spiky talons, not to mention delivering some well-aimed pecks and scratches that would hurt, but not ultimately cause any serious or permanent damage. Though Dion had summoned protection, he was not a killer. His intention had only been to delay his attackers, and teach them a hard lesson in the process. Right now, all of that appeared to be going rather well and according to plan.

Leaving the birds to do their job, Dion locked the doors to secure the house. On his return to the front room, he was happy to find that Olivia, who, though shaken and bruised, was not seriously hurt. Now, she was smiling, amused by the ridiculous spectacle as Dion, pleased with the success of his feathered tactics, joined her by the window. Had the situation not been so desperate, it might even have been funny.

Shade was frantically muttering a special Dark Star incantation to cause a malevolent electrical storm, but could not concentrate for fighting off the beating wings and sharp beaks. He needed both of his arms for protection and incantation gestures were impossible. For a minute, a jet-black cloud appeared on the horizon, but disappeared again as soon as he lost contact. The light and magic Dion and Olivia had built around Oaklands from many years of communion with the Lumerin proved just too strong a barrier.

The unfortunate men were chased round and round at the front of the house, unable to get to their car for a good half hour due to the constant assaults. Sid, Jack and Barry picked up stones to throw at the birds but missed every time. Occasionally, they were allowed to get within a couple of feet of their vehicle, but just when they felt secure, the assaults would begin all over again until they were exhausted from running and flailing. Finally, when Dion decided that it was safe, he opened the window and whistled to call off his fighting birds. Battered and exhausted, the four men were allowed to creep into their Jag and crawl off down the drive, covered in feathers and bird droppings.

"Bloody birds!" wailed Sid, dabbing blood from his scratched face. "I'll hate them forever. I'll ring their scrawny necks…. I'll stuff the lot of them into feather pillows!"

Whilst Barry and Jack made weak, painful attempts to laugh

at Sid, Hugo, silent and beaten, kept his mouth shut about the severe damage to his clothes and his pride as he drove away from the Order of Lumen. He had not expected them to be so powerful. He had not, in his wildest dreams, imagined being attacked by a hawk man and a regiment of winged nightmares. The unspeakable humiliation had made Shade more dangerous than ever. Someone was going to pay.

12 MAGIC AND MOONLIGHT

As they sped away from Oaklands and the multitudes of screeching birds, Toby's instincts and newly discovered abilities made him certain that the commotion would delay their pursuers.

"I think it'll be a good half hour before they get out of there," he informed the others as a big triumphant smirk took over his face.

"I suppose you got privileged information about that from one of your feathered friends, then," chuckled Gabriel.

"You could say that, I got it from a raven I spotted on the gate post."

"You're so useful these days, much more than you used to be," laughed Daisy, teasing.

"Cheek!" Toby pulled his cousin's hair from the back seat.

"Calm down, will you!" Gabriel tried stern soothing tactics. "I know all this high anxiety has made you both boisterous, but if your information's correct, Toby, and we really do have only half an hour, then I need to concentrate on getting us as far away as possible from Hugo Shade."

Toby and Daisy settled back in their seats whilst Gabriel directed all his attention at the road, putting his foot down as much as possible, with no intention of stopping until they reached their new destination. Their instructions from the

Lumerin were to continue west, following a prescribed route. Gabriel knew that meant at least another two hours of driving, but his ability to keep his mind in the present, and his intent to keep Daisy and Toby safe, would enable him to reach his goal. Keeping this certainty in his mind and in his heart, he was able to relax. "Thanks to Dion," he said, "we're blessed with a full tank of petrol and as there's absolutely no sign of Shade's Jaguar at that moment, I think an advantage has been won."

The farm worker's cottage, set back from the road behind a high hedge and some way up the cart track leading to a farm, was almost impossible to spot from the road. Tall, wild parsley, spilling abundantly from the sides of the track into the meadow beyond, mingled with buttercups, foxgloves and purple tufted vetch, to create a palette of colour which added to the camouflage by drawing the eye away from the direction of the modest dwelling. Gabriel tooted the horn twice.

Seth Meadows, who had been on full alert waiting for his visitors all morning, leapt to his feet with a sigh of relief.

Seth lived alone in this simple cottage because he loved peace and quiet and the big farm- house was just too noisy and hectic with his brother Simon's large boisterous family. Greeting his guests warmly, he ushered them all into his cozy sitting room where cool lemonade and sandwiches were already set out on the table under a white linen cloth. The pale yellow walls and the soft green three-piece suite reminded Daisy of daffodils.

"Now," said Seth, taking over. "You two sit and eat while Gabriel and I get your luggage from the car, and then I'll drive it up to the farm and hide it in the barn where it'll be out of sight. I'm afraid you'll have to continue on foot for a while now, but I'm sure that the Order of Lumen will be able to provide you with appropriate transport when the journey demands it. All the information to help you will, of course, be given to all the right people at the right time."

Enjoying the sandwiches, Toby found himself being watched intently by Seth's Border collie, Bess, who had been left to guard the house. Her tail thumped the floor as her liquid brown eyes held him hostage. Toby heard her say, "Give us some of your food."

"Oh, okay, then," he replied out loud, reluctantly breaking off a bit of his cheese sandwich and handing it over. It was swallowed in a single gulp and the plea renewed until Toby complied.

"Don't be so soft with her," laughed Seth, returning just in time to spot Toby's plight with Bess.

"I've always been a sucker for begging dogs." Toby quickly put the rest of his sandwich into his own mouth. He had the impression that Bess was laughing at him, though in a friendly way, of course. He was not offended and loved this connection to the animal kingdom. It made him feel strong, more like the person he wanted to be. A sense of contentment settled on him. He had nothing to prove to anyone.

* * * *

As the barn doors closed on the Morris Traveller, four disgruntled people in a black Jaguar car passed by Seth's cottage without even a glance at the cart track or the wild flowers. Hugo Shade was keen to find an inn so that he could wash, change his clothes and dab some antiseptic on his scratches and pecks. He saw no beauty in nature and had little time for it. As far as he was concerned, nature was something to avoid because it was either messy like pigs or hostile like the awful birds. Thinking about the birds just made him wince with pain and embarrassment.

Hugo was heading for a place known as Fairwater Lake, but feeling fresh and normal again after the attacks at Oaklands had become his first priority. He reasoned that kids would need to eat and that Greenway would not be keen to head across open country on foot in daylight. There was, so far, no sign of the Morris Traveller. It was as though it had just disappeared. Still, Hugo believed with an arrogant certainty that he was right about the daylight, and after checking his journal, he knew that sunset would happen at nine twenty-one and that it would be dark about ten. That is when he would be ready to attack, armed with suitable incantations to call down the wrath of Dark Star in an evil storm as soon as the opportunity presented itself.

Hungry, cross and tired, Sid, Jack and Barry, still hurting from the bird ordeal, were somewhat relieved to hear Shade's plans to take a break. Even Jack had little strength to be awkward and the thought of a nap in lovely clean sheets had become quite tantalizing. All of this considered, when the Old Swan Inn appeared around the next bend, the mood in the car lifted.

* * * *

Back at the cottage, Gabriel, Seth and the children were deep in conversation with Seth explaining the travel arrangements.

"I think you should stay here for the Lantern Ceremony up at the farm and then set off immediately after sunset, which, I think, is about half nine. We'll get any information we need and then I'll be able to lead you across country to Fairwater Lake. It ought to take us just over half an hour."

"That sounds absolutely right to me," agreed Gabriel nodding.

"Why a lake?" asked Daisy becoming curious. "What's there?"

"Ynys Arian, the Isle of Silver," replied Seth, his expression soft and dreamy. "I know for certain that it exists, though I've never seen it in my whole life."

"What do you mean?" Toby frowned, looking puzzled.

Seth continued as his guests gave him their full attention. "Most people think it's a myth, a fairy story, but I know that some members of our Order, who sought its wisdom, have both seen it and been allowed to go there."

"Have you been there, Gabriel?" Toby was intrigued.

"No, because as yet, I've had no need. I believe Morag is a regular visitor, though I can't tell you why. She has powerful connections to its three female guardians through her exceptional second sight and ability to change the appearance of things."

"Is Morag one of your top people then?" Daisy asked.

"You could say that. Morag's always there at the beginning and ending of any great change or event, recording everything of significance within the Order of Lumen. She's one of our most respected elders, though she'd never tell you that herself. We believe the three Sisters of Arian to be about as close as you can get to the first Lumerin who came to our world and it is widely thought that Morag, who's learned much from them, can walk between worlds of her own accord as they do."

At this point in the conversation, the nerves in Daisy's skin had begun to prickle, causing goose bumps and shivers. "I can't wait," she said, trying to sound normal, "it feels as though I'm entering another dream, melting into the mists of Lumenorian legend. It's frightening and exciting all at the same time."

During the nine o'clock Lantern Ceremony the companions were told the whereabouts of a rowing boat hidden in the reeds on the bank of Fairwater Lake and that a messenger would be waiting for them.

They left the cottage around nine forty carrying their rucksacks containing clothes, torches, compasses, drinking water and a small pack of Gabriel's new potions. Daisy took a quick look at the blue stone in her belt bag to check it was still there. Seth's instructions were to show them the way to the lake and then to return home once he had seen them safely onto the water.

Although the moon had just entered its third quarter, the silver-white light was incredibly bright, aided by the millions of stars spread across the midnight blue sky. Illuminated wild parsley lined their path through the meadow in ghostly profusion. The effect was magical. Breathing in the pure, warm air, the children became energized, happy and poised on the brink of a great adventure. Infused with the light from the sky and the Lumerin, there was a feeling of safety, regardless of their unpleasant memories of Hugo Shade or distant echoes of Maxwell Delano. The night birds and animals called to Toby, acknowledging his welcome presence in their kingdom. It seemed as though the land itself was on their side.

* * * *

And perhaps it was, because Hugo Shade, in spite of his attempts at perfection and efficiency had taken a nap and - miraculously - overslept in his starched white sheets, so by the time he had dressed in his new Amori shirt and crisply pressed trousers, Toby, Daisy and Gabriel had already set off across the fields.

* * * *

After trekking for what seemed like ages - but without feeling tired - the meadow beyond the final stile dissolved into the water of a vast, deep lake. Seth led them along the bank to find the rowing boat conveniently moored and hidden in the reeds. An owl hooted from the shadow of a tree as a coot flapped through the undergrowth to sail in the shallows.

Close to the bank, a grey heron, poised on one steady leg, eyed them curiously as they moved towards the boat.

"Where's the guide, then?" Daisy asked, expecting someone to be waiting for them.

"Zip it, Daise!" Toby was concentrating on the heron. "This bird wants to talk to me."

Daisy backed off. She hadn't yet quite got the hang of the fact that guides did not necessarily have to be human.

Toby listened, still and attentive. "She wants us to get into the boat and row in that direction. Toby pointed up the lake to his left. "She'll fly in front of us."

"This is where I leave you, " said Seth. "It's your task, not mine. I've brought you here, as instructed, and I know you'll be safe now."

"Goodbye, old friend, and thank you," said Gabriel, "We'll meet again - you can count on that."

As the boat left the shallows with Gabriel at the oars, the heron leapt into the air, looking like some prehistoric shadow flying before them into the night. For a few moments, a passing cloud left only the light of the stars reflected in the silken water, but then… there it was, bathed in silver. The cloud had released the light of the waning moon to reveal a shimmering island rising out of the lake in a place that had previously been an empty space. Gabriel was so stunned to be sailing into the heart of this mythical landscape that he almost dropped an oar.

"Ynys Arian!" he cried, ecstatic. " Our need has been met!"

* * * *

At the same time, an irate Hugo Shade, having arrived only that minute on the shore of the lake, stood dumbfounded, gazing hopelessly at what he took to be a vanishing rowing boat. He could see no more as the mist descended and shut him out forever. He had no legitimate need.

13 THE THREE SISTERS

Once the rowing boat had been safely moored on the tiny, reed-choked beach, the heron, her task complete, returned to her own business of searching for fish in the shallows. Outlined in moonlight, a weathered wooden staircase extended upwards, leading the companions away from the water to the land above, where a single, chalky pathway wound its way across a grassy space towards an uneven stone wall.

Above the studded gate, three brass bells hung from an arch. The central, largest one, attached to a rope, invoked a silent invitation to pull. Toby couldn't resist and grabbed it with enthusiasm, pulling as hard as possible. The result was a loud clanging. "Okay, okay, Toby that's enough I'm sure they heard you." Gabriel to put his hands over his ears to block out the din.

They didn't have to wait long before the clanging was answered by a woman whose face was as smooth and black as a polished obsidian stone. Her jet- black hair, styled in braids, was decorated with a variety of rainbow beads and a pair of clear smiling eyes reflected the warmth and depth of a sunlit pool. Simply dressed in a full-length, sky blue robe, she looked comfortable and statuesque. Daisy could not shake off a feeling that she had met the woman somewhere before, even though logic told her it was impossible.

"I am Asha." She sounded like brown velvet. "You cannot imagine just how long my sisters and I have waited for this moment."

As she hugged them one by one, they felt a sense of belonging. It was a most special welcome, like coming home after a long absence, into the loving presence of the Lumerin, except that this person was a solid human being. "Toby and Daisy, our Harp Children... and Gabriel, who has so much responsibility. Brave, reliable Gabriel, I have always known that you would be the right person."

The dwelling behind the wall was a substantial, single-storey log cabin constructed from cedar wood. In the centre of the small courtyard, summer flowers trailed from terracotta pots and a border planted with scented shrubs circled the wall, overloading their senses with the sweetest aromas of jasmine, rose and honeysuckle, mingling in the moonlight with the woodiness of the house.

The other two sisters, dressed in identical sky blue garments, came out to greet their guests. Slender and full of life, they were all beautiful, but no one, on first acquaintance, would ever have assumed that these three women were in any way related

Here was Tara, coffee-skinned and raven-haired, with almond eyes, whose appearance was so oriental, whilst Olwen, with her golden red waves, ivory complexion and china blue eyes reminded Daisy of a picture she had seen in the 'Treasury of Celtic Tales' on her Grandad Evans' bookshelf.

"I see what you are thinking." Olwen was reading their minds.

"A feeling of family can be a mysterious inner connection you have with someone, a link which is neither dependent on bloodline nor background. We are sisters because, deep down, we three are Lumerin, a bond going far beyond this realm into dimensions only the most wise could ever comprehend.

"We have long been the Keepers of the Island," continued Asha, "which has been here since the beginning of time, existing in this world, and also beyond it. Our purpose is to serve you and assist your quest. If you fail and the connection to the Lumerin is broken, we may never be found again in this dimension, as shadows drive the light out of Lumenor."

Pondering on those words in serious silence, Gabriel and the children followed the sisters into the house.

The welcoming smell of cedar immediately filled their nostrils cheering them and bringing them back into the moment. There was little conventional furniture in the main room, but it was certainly bright and interesting. Piles of patterned cushions in sumptuous silken fabrics were scattered around three low, wooden tables inlaid with marble mosaics in spiral patterns. Tapestries and carvings adorned the walls, depicting animals, birds, trees, small human figures, suns, moons and starry constellations. It was the kind of room that Daisy would have loved for herself, although, until now, she could never have had the imagination to dream it up.

As the visitors seated themselves on the welcoming cushions, Asha brought refreshments on a tray. Toby enjoyed his honey cake with eager delight, whilst Daisy sipped elderflower water politely from an elegant silver tumbler and ate her fresh strawberries and cream. Gabriel, quiet and a little stunned, allowed a few quiet tears of gratitude to well up in the corners of his eyes and splash onto his cheeks when nobody was looking. For a moment, he could let go of his enormous responsibility and feel like a child himself.

That night, they slept soundly on rolled out mattresses in a plain room, waking only when the first gentle rays of sunlight filtered through the fine white muslin curtains. The sound of birdsong and buzzing honey- bees outside, welcomed in another warm day on the Silver Isle.

"I think that this weather will last for a while," announced Tara, "and today is the first day of Greening, when the light is at its brightest. I am glad that you are here at this time because I think that it will be most beneficial and auspicious for your quest."

"We're safe again." Daisy was happy, "it's just so good to be somewhere that's invisible to the majority of the population of Lumenor. There's no way that Hugo Shade or Sid Planks would ever be allowed to see this island, so, at least for the time being, we're free. Even so I won't remove the pouch containing the Stone of Peace and Inspiration from my belt bag, just in case a moment of carelessness I forget it when the time comes to leave."

The sisters who grew their own vegetables, fruit and herbs also kept some livestock for milk, cheese and wool. There was plentiful fresh water from an underground spring, which never ran dry and beehives like the ones in Morag's cottage garden. Hunger and thirst would never visit this place, though a person might starve if they could not see it.

Toby decided not to think about leaving, but to get on with living in this atmosphere of complete security. It was the kind of safety he had always felt as a small child. Ynys Arian has just that kind of effect on you.

The Lantern Ceremony, held at twilight on the first day of Greening, was particularly magical. In addition to the central golden hue, lights of all colours appeared in tones, which were both at the same time soft and bright, swirling and whirling… all in the dusk of the longest day.

Once the lantern was ablaze, Tara opened a simple wooden box to reveal another soft leather pouch, which she solemnly handed to Toby.

"Open it, Toby," she instructed.

Fulfilling the request, Toby withdrew a deep red stone from the leather folds. It was exactly the same shape and size as the blue one. Examining the jewel was like being enfolded in a soft, warm cloak or encircled by a protective ring of fire. The more they all looked at it, the safer they felt.

"This is the Stone of Protection," said Olwen

"Thanks," replied Toby, feeling the weight of the responsibility sparkling in the palm of his hand. "I won't let you down," he added, mesmerized by the warm red depths of the Stone of Protection.

"I know you will not, Toby," whispered Asha, "and nor will any of you," she added, looking at Gabriel and Daisy. "In all my years and you can't imagine just how long that is, I have never ceased to be amazed at the way people strengthen and rally in a crisis, with a common aim to stand up to a threat and you three have certainly reinforced my faith in humankind. Where such character and courage exist, there will always be a way to overcome. In my own heart, I have never been more certain."

The time passed slowly in a mood of calm happiness and continued sunshine. There was hardly a cloud in the sky for about fifteen days as the young people's minds and bodies grew strong and healthy in the care of the sisters and the magical air of Ynys Arian, so far away from the stress and present danger of the world outside.

They busied themselves, helping with the butter and cheese making, as well as learning to collect honey. Toby talked to the bees and the goats, whilst Daisy sketched and Gabriel listened to each of the sisters in turn, benefitting from their enormous store of wisdom. This was a unique experience in a rare and magical environment for all three.

Then, one day, Gabriel called the cousins to pass on some news. "We shall be leaving before the full moon of the twenty-ninth day of Greening, and we must make preparations for our departure in three days' time."

By now, neither Toby nor Daisy had any idea what day of the season it was. The past and future had all faded leaving only a contented, present time. It was going to be a terrible wrench to break away from this invisible island with its mysterious sisters, but because they all felt stronger, any careless mention of Maxwell Delano failed to cause the slightest fear.

They left Ynys Arian as they had arrived, in a boat guided by a grey heron, on an overcast morning with fresh provisions in their rucksacks and new courage in their intention to succeed. As the island gradually faded and vanished behind a curtain of mist rising from the depths of the lake, the companions knew for certain that its magic had changed them inside.

"It's gone," moaned Toby, gazing back at the empty expanse of water. "I wanted to stay there forever."

"Ah, yes." Gabriel's reply was comforting. "You're not alone in that, but Ynys Arian and the sisters are still right here, in your heart, and if you're quiet and listen carefully, you might just hear them sometimes when you need their advice."

Toby placed his hand gently on his chest, with every hope that what Gabriel had told him was true. It wouldn't be the last time he would look for the Silver Isle in his imagination.

Guided by the heron, they moored the boat in an entirely different location at the other end of the lake, where Seth Meadows awaited their return, according to his own instructions from the Lumerin.

"We must be on our way," he whispered with some urgency. "I've been keeping an eye on the area around the lake for the past week, and, sure enough only yesterday morning, I discovered three horrible men camping out near the bank where you left. I didn't like the look of them, so I hid in the bushes to see what they were up to. A smart, black bloke turned up... I couldn't hear what was being said but there was a bit of an argument between him and one of the others before they all sat down, staring at the water. I must say I felt uncomfortable – no, more than that – I felt threatened."

"Well, that's definitely Hugo Shade, Sid Planks and Sid's two friends," confirmed Gabriel. "Did you see a black Jaguar car, Seth?" he asked as an afterthought.

"Sure did," Seth was absolutely certain. "It's been in the lanes around the lake a lot. I followed Shade back to it. Nice car."

Daisy pulled a face. "Nice car - but foul people. What are we going to do now?"

"As far as I know," reasoned Seth, "they're all still where I last saw them, about half a mile away and my own car is about ten minutes' walk in the opposite direction. I intend to take you to the station at Fairwater Junction so that you can catch the next train. If we hurry, we can be away long before they realize what's happened."

"Sounds like a plan," said Toby without asking any questions about the rail destination. "Come on, let's go."

They hurried away, unaware that Hugo Shade had left Fairwater Lake the night before and was, at that moment, miles away from there. That very evening, obediently following instructions, Hugo Shade had conducted his own simple Dark Star Ceremony, using a small very tarnished lantern, a special parting gift from Max to be kept in the boot of the Jag pending further notice. Then, armed with new orders, he had decided to leave immediately. In future, Shade wouldn't need to make so many calls from inns and phone boxes, because he had been given direct contact. It was a risk Delano felt he had to take, to save time.

As they arrived at Fairwater Junction Gabriel Daisy and Toby had no idea that a hostile reception had already been planned for them at Broom Hill.

14 TREES

At Fairwater Junction, three cautious passengers boarded the ten o'clock train to the south coast with tickets Seth had booked in advance. Walking warily towards the rear of the train, they eventually found an empty compartment, filling the vacant seats with their rucksacks to claim the entire space as their own. A quick glance into every other compartment as he passed had reassured Gabriel that Hugo Shade and his three nasty pals were definitely not on the train.

With sighs of relief, all three relaxed into the comfortable grey and red striped seats to enjoy the view from the window. After all, to Toby and Daisy, this was a completely different world, even though much of the landscape was reminiscent of places in Britain. Since their visit to Morag, they expected to see things that seemed familiar in Lumenor, though indeed, things weren't always what they seemed.

The Stone of Protection was now safely stowed in the leather bag threaded on to Toby's belt. He patted it confidently, enjoying a clear memory of Ynys Arian.

"How long's this journey, Gabriel?" he asked.

"Not totally sure, but I think it's about an hour and a half. It's the first stop after Crixton. I believe it's one of those market towns in the middle of nowhere. Still, there'll be someone to meet us."

"Not so bad, then," Daisy added, joining in the conversation. "I wonder what happened to those Dark Star creeps? Do you suppose they've realized that we've left the island?'

"Try not to speculate," replied Gabriel. "Dreaming up different scenarios will keep your mind connected to Hugo Shade, and that could make you anxious. Let's deal with them when we have to, and try to enjoy the time in between."

"It's a deal," she said, pushing away a sudden, ugly image of Sid Planks and replacing it with a more pleasant one of the three sisters. Daisy was experiencing less difficulty switching her thoughts to positive things since her visit to Ynys Arian and she hoped that this small breakthrough would continue, though her instincts told her that she still had a long way to go on that score.

"What's in the rucksacks, then?" asked Toby, beginning to think about his stomach.

"Homemade cheese, bread, honey cakes, elderflower water and apples." Gabriel put his own backpack on the floor took out a small selection of goodies and placed them on the seat beside him.

"It couldn't be better - almost a couple of hours of relaxation, magical food from Ynys Arian to feed the spirit as well as nourish the body, and the best company in Lumenor. What else could a man ask for?"

They were all surprisingly relaxed as villages, fields, distant hills and rivers hurtled by at speed, disappearing from view as though they had never existed. It was all over much too soon as the train slowed down before pulling into the station at Broom Hill.

The dove grey sky held the promise of a refreshing shower, which would have been welcome rather than inconvenient, as the air was humid and a little sticky. Alert as always, Gabriel opened the door to scan the platform for possible enemies before alighting. So far, so good, and except for a short, stocky man with a weathered face and unkempt hair like straw, there was definitely no one else on the platform.

Gabriel had recognized him immediately as Eddie Meadows, a cousin of Seth's, a Shire horse breeder in that part of the country. The resemblance to Seth was uncanny. A quick greeting was followed by an equally speedy exit from the station because Eddie, who had a sense of foreboding he couldn't shake off, was keen to leave as soon as possible. Clambering into his jeep, they were all glad to be back on the road again.

"We'll go back to my place for a rest, and then I'll take you to The Sanctuary later. We can travel in the jeep as far as the wood and afterwards you'll be on foot. I'll drop you at the shortest and most direct path, so it won't take you more than twenty minutes."

"What's The Sanctuary then?" Daisy was intrigued.

"It's a place hardly anybody ever goes to, because hardly anybody knows where it is," said Eddie. "It's been a safe place for the Order of Lumen for years. I can remember first hearing about it from my grandfather when I was a boy. It's got some kind of magic that keeps it hidden from Dark Star, or anybody else with harmful intentions, for that matter. That's why it's called The Sanctuary."

Before anyone could say another word, the sleek black Jaguar pulled out from the side of the road and blocked their way. The tyres of the jeep screeched as Eddie slammed on the brakes, swiftly putting the gears into reverse and backing up with as much speed as he could towards a farm gate. Beyond it, an empty level field stretched away towards the wood in the distance.

"Go!" he shouted. "Run for the trees! "

Fired by the urgency in Eddie's voice, they jumped out, throwing their rucksacks on to their backs as they hurtled through the gate into the field. The exertion was hot and uncomfortable, but the danger of capture was far worse. Without looking back, they ran for it. The only thing that mattered now was to go forward and escape. Of course, the black Jag arrived only a minute behind them, but lacking the benefits of a stay on Ynys Arian, its occupants were neither as fit nor as fast.

As Barry jumped out of the car, his first instinct was to grab hold of Eddie Meadows, but Jack pulled him away, realizing that there simply wasn't enough time to take any extra hostages.

"I won't forget you." Hugo Shade pointed menacingly at Eddie, whilst attempting to sprint through the gate in his unsuitable, polished shoes. Eddie, glaring at Hugo's back, stood his ground by the jeep. He needed to be certain that Gabriel and the youngsters reached their destination before he left and knew there was little point in joining in the chase. There would be no need of any outside help once his friends had entered the wood. Tense and anxious, Eddie waited.

With their pursuers less than a hundred yards sprint behind them, Toby leapt into the sheltering trees, followed closely by Daisy and Gabriel. Landing in the undergrowth, they encountered an unexpected but very welcome cool breeze after the grey humidity of the open field. A mysterious breeze, which soon became swirls of green, enveloping all three of them in a strange cloak of light, in which could be seen hints of leaf and pine needle, berry and cone.

"It's the trees!" Toby experienced a sudden realization. "They're helping us. We must go deeper into the wood."

And as they ran, it seemed like the air was giving them a gentle, supportive push, through the leaf shapes dancing and playing around them.

There was no sign of Hugo Shade, but they could hear him like a harsh echo against the soft touch of the green breeze.

"Where are you, Planks, you idiot?"

"I can't see," came the distressed reply. "It's all gone bloody green. Where've Jack and Barry gone?"

"Over here," answered Jack, who, having lost all sense of direction, believed that he was being suffocated by hundreds of leaves. "And don't call us idiots, Shady, or I'll make you sorry!" Jack's constant state of anger with Hugo Shade had a knack of taking his mind off everything else, even his own safety.

"Arrgghh!" ... There was no reply other than the scream of

pain, because Shade was being whipped back to the edge of the wood by stinging, invisible branches as he tried to spit out the leaves that kept filling his mouth. Somebody was throwing fir cones at him as he tumbled over and over, out of the trees. He landed, winded and bruised, sprawling flat on his back in the field.

The other three were also blown out by a whirling green hurricane, ripping their breath away. Arms flailing, they too landed heavily and painfully, one by one, on the ground beside Hugo. Their treatment, though unpleasant, had been a little less harsh, because the tree spirits always dealt with people according to the amount of kindness or malice they held, and that is why no Dark Star could ever enter Sanctuary Wood.

Daisy stumbled, twisting her ankle badly, an unfortunate mishap, which quickly put paid to their flight. Gabriel picked her up and, placing one arm around her waist, helped her to hop.

"It really hurts Gabriel, I have to stop."

Toby was silent, listening. "They've been chucked out of the wood and they won't be let back in. They're well and truly barred so it's okay, we can stop now. It's safe."

"Are you really talking to the trees?" asked Daisy in disbelief as Gabriel found a convenient tree stump for her to sit on. She screwed up her face in the stabbing pain caused by the injury.

"Course I am," Toby was happy. "The prophecy says that I can communicate with all living beings – remember? It doesn't specify human beings yeah or even animal beings, for that matter."

"The trees are alive, Daisy," Gabriel explained, taking one of the special potions he had made at Oaklands from a box stowed in his rucksack. "The trees are not just things you know, they are friends." Using the dropper from the blue glass bottle, he let a small amount of the potion fall onto Daisy's bruised ankle.

"It's a rapid healer. An injury like this can take days to mend, forcing you to slow down and rest, but since our time's limited, we need to be getting on. The Lumerin gave instructions to make it for our journey because accidents can happen more easily when you're in a hurry. We should have stopped immediately the breeze came. It's my fault. In the rush, I'd forgotten about the presence of the tree spirits - I was careless and I let my mind get caught up in the panic... Does that feel better?"

After only five minutes, Daisy was back on her feet, picking up her rucksack. " That's amazing Gabriel! What next Toby?"

Toby closed his eyes and listened again. "Follow the path to the centre of the wood, don't go right or left, just stay on the path."

Half an hour later, they walked out of the trees into an enormous clearing at the centre of the wood, a large, grassy space with woodland all around its circumference. The sky, framed by the treetops, formed a pale grey arena above them, and the still air felt humid again. Pigeons flapped and cooed around the wooden veranda of a ramshackle cottage on the other side of the grove, whilst smaller, unseen birds hidden in the foliage sang their individual melodies.

Strolling in silence around the clearing, they discovered a sweet spring bubbling up from the earth into an ancient stone basin, where it overflowed to form a rivulet meandering into the trees. Somewhere, it would become a stream before it widened into a river and finally gushed into the sea. The space was alive with natural, harmonious sounds.

After washing their faces in the spring, they made their way to the centre of the clearing, marked by a single, tall standing stone. It was a curious object on which unfamiliar symbols had been carved.

"You are looking at Ancient Lumen script," Gabriel explained, "it's inviting those with a good heart to rest a while and be safe."

"My heart isn't good... I'm having angry feelings about Hugo Shade and those three vile men." Daisy looked worried as she traced the symbols on the stone with the index finger of her right hand.

"Perfectly understandable," said Gabriel, "but you wouldn't set out to obliterate them even though they might want to obliterate you. It is hatred that destroys you know, not ordinary, justified anger. You can teach someone a lesson without destroying them."

Daisy thought about it, "I suppose that I only get seriously angry when someone is cruel and really pushes me around, but now I think about it, I don't believe it would ever occur to me to deliberately harm someone ... would it? ..."

"That's why we all like you so much Daisy and I'm sure that you would have no problem getting approval from whoever carved those words on the stone. Respect! - You're our youngest Healer of Souls."

Daisy began to like herself a little more, smiling as she remembered how Dion had taught Shade a severe lesson with the birds, and that was important, because he had managed to defeat a dangerous enemy without actually becoming like him. She and the others had also escaped as a result of his genius planning. "The Order of Lumen – it's just the best."

They were about to explore the cottage they had noticed before the distraction of the standing stone, when they heard a light tenor voice behind them

"I see that you've found The Sanctuary."

They sky finally gave in, letting the welcome rain shower fall into the thirsty woodland.

15 THE SANCTUARY

Running across the open grove, Rafael Santos led the way towards the covered cottage veranda, which offered both shelter, and chairs to sit on. They reached the decking only just in time to escape a very heavy downpour.

Safe and dry, Gabriel was shaking hands with a man he obviously knew, a man with shoulder length, deep brown hair, clear matching eyes and coppery complexion. Rafael's appearance was delicate and comfortable in green trousers, calico shirt and worn brown sandals. The slim, artistic fingers, fine boned feet and open expression suggested a gentle temperament, which Toby and Daisy both liked.

The storm, though brief, had poured much needed water into the parched earth, cooling the vast canopy of leaves and purifying the dusty air with a sharp scent of wet greenery. The rain had brought welcome relief and refreshment to all life in the woodland.

"Well, we didn't get to see Eddie's Shire horses," complained Toby, "but at least we got here without being captured."

Gabriel nodded, looking relieved.

"Who created The Sanctuary and what's it all about then?" Daisy wondered if she had just stumbled into yet another legend.

Rafael seemed to know a lot about it. "The Sanctuary was

founded long ago, by two of the first Lumerin to walk this world in human form. The standing stone was erected and carved by Lord Lanto and the spring created by Narda, the white lady of the grove. They say that it bubbled up where she was standing and still sings her praises all the way to the sea. Together, they made a pact with the tree spirits that this place would offer protection to all who deserved it. This is very old woodland and although for most, the Sanctuary is only a story nowadays, it's certainly a true one, for I am its keeper."

"And by the way," Gabriel added, "the water's supposed to give long life and strength."

"We'd better drink some of that, then." Daisy liked the idea that she might live longer.

"The lemonade you're drinking is made from it," Rafael was enthusiastic.

"Test it out, Daise," joked Toby. "See if you can lift Gabriel."

"No way!' Gabriel put up his hands to ward her off. "I don't think it can work so quickly. The effect probably grows over time with a great deal of water."

The atmosphere was fun and light-hearted amongst the friendly trees, as they continued to drink their long-life lemonade.

"I am descended from a long line of Sanctuary Guardians," explained Rafael, "and my son Rowan will follow in my footsteps. It is a sacred tradition."

"Where is your son?" Daisy always had a genuine interest in people's relatives. It was a trait she had inherited from her Welsh grandmother.

"With my wife, Violetta, and his twin sister, Willow." Rafael felt pleased to be asked. "We have another home in Broom Hill, where my children go to school and where Violetta and I are known as professional musicians. I'm a singer/song writer and my wife's an accomplished pianist. I'm here whenever I'm needed. As you can imagine, this magical place is also my own personal sanctuary, and a great source of inspiration for my work. The family's coming in a couple of days, when the kids break up from school for the long Greening holiday."

"That's really cool." Toby was thinking how much fun it would be to see some other young people. Gabriel was such a great bloke, but just a bit too old to be into exploring, climbing trees and making a lot of noise.

Rafael reached into his pocket and drew out a brown leather pouch. "I'm instructed to put this into your safe keeping, Gabriel," he said. "This is the Stone of Good Health."

The pale, translucent jewel was a mixture of delicate greens and blues, like the ocean that washes the white, sandy shores of the Western Isles. It seemed to reflect the airy blue of the sky and the watery green of the sea, but never one more than the other.

As Daisy fell under its subtle spell, she had an impression of a golden harp in a hall of rosy marble, where aquamarine waves crashed outside tall, bright windows. "The Hall of Awen," she whispered, as though in a trance.

"Ah, you saw it, too," replied Rafael, picking up a guitar which he strummed as he began to sing in a faraway voice.

In the Beautiful Realm, within my heart of stars,
The dancing sun shines bright, upon the Hall of Awen
And a harp of gold plays songs of peace.

The melody enchanted and enticed them into stunning landscapes, deep within their imaginations and they were silent then, as there seemed to be nothing left to say.

When the song was ended, Gabriel replaced the gem in its pouch, and put it into the empty bag on his belt. He had another responsibility now, in addition to ensuring the children's safety and the success of their quest. There was still a long way to go. *It's just as well I'm a level headed sort of chap,* he thought, breathing deeply into the present moment to ground himself. *Well, at least most of the time.*

Rustic and fairly basic, the cottage provided enough for their needs with adequate beds, and simple food foraged from the forest, or grown in the small garden behind the cottage. Water came in plentiful supply from Narda's spring and Rafael made good bread, cakes and pies with ingredients brought from Broom Hill. There was nothing else to need or to want.

As the warm weather continued with the occasional cooling shower, all meals were eaten outside on the veranda where Toby had attracted three plump wood pigeons, which constantly pestered him. He assumed that the pigeons thought he must be an easy target, as they strutted around pushing out their chests and cooing. "Crumbs, crumbs, give us crumbs."

The evenings were a real source of pleasure, with Rafael entertaining with his flute or, singing songs and strumming his guitar. They learned the choruses and joined in when appropriate. *For anyone receptive and willing to participate even in the smallest measure, music can create great happiness or soothe the soul and drive dark shadows from the mind,* Gabriel thought as he watched Daisy and Toby enjoying themselves. *Rock on Raf - the kids are having so much fun. It's good stuff and I love it!*

One evening, Toby wandered away from the company, drawn into the trees by the lonely hooting of a night bird. Following the eerie sound of two hoots followed by a short silence, then another two, he came across an awesome eagle owl perched in a frame of leaves on a low branch. The orange eyes, glinting like hot coals, pulled him closer. Sensing a great friendliness from the bird, Toby spoke. "I'll call you Two Hoots," he decided, wishing that he were tall enough to reach up and stroke the tawny feathers.

"Fair enough," replied the owl. "I have come to remind you that there is still danger ahead, even though it is quite safe now and will be so until you have found the next stone - but take note, my friend, that there are sure to be enemies watching and that the big city is not such an easy place."

"What big city?" Toby was apprehensive.

"The capital of Lumenor, of course. Be sure to take good care of the girl. I will spread messages. Never despair - you will always find an ally."

And with that, the owl flew into the night, hooting his way

towards the starry sky, leaving Toby to wander back to the others, puzzling over the bird's warning. He decided to think about it for a while, and tell Gabriel later.

"Talking to owls, I suppose," teased Daisy on Toby's return.

"You could say that." Toby forced a smile.

Violetta and the twins came for several visits during their time in The Sanctuary. Toby and Daisy especially enjoyed the company because Rowan and Willow who were only a year younger were able to tell them more about life in Lumenor from their point of view as well as exploring the wood and discovering the hideouts of its creatures. They climbed trees, learned to track, drank water from the spring and picked up a little more Ancient Lumen. Life became natural, a little on the wild side and the freedom to roam was fantastic.

One day when all the family were there, Rafael brought his guitar out after lunch. "We're going to teach you The Lumerinda. It's the song for calling the Lumerin in the old language, and you need to know it."

"Epic!" Daisy jumped up from her seat. "I can remember bits of it, but I'd love to be able to sing it all."

"Okay," said Rafael, "so when you've learned it, you must practice, because the Lumerin say that it may be necessary for your future wellbeing."

"If it's necessary for our wellbeing, that must mean some kind of problem and then we'll be forced to sing it, though I can't see how that could help." Nevertheless, Toby was just as keen to learn the song as Daisy. They it mastered it in double quick time with a little help from another of Gabriel's special potions called Remember Me.

The four young people spent the rest of the afternoon until sunset, singing in the woods accompanied by all sorts of birds as the trees waved their top branches in appreciation.

During the Lantern Ceremony in the cottage garden, Toby and Daisy sang their hearts out, and because they could join in, the experience was even more amazing than their first encounter with the Lumerin at Morag's. This time, they made their own personal contact and realized how good it felt to play a full part in an Order of Lumen Ceremony. They were no longer observers with an unexpected, scary task because they were, in fact, becoming connected.

"We're going soon," announced Daisy later, on the veranda.

"Tomorrow," said Toby with certainty.

"To the coast," continued Rafael

"Eddie Meadows is driving us," added Gabriel.

"To seek the Stone of Happiness," concluded Daisy.

Rafael began to laugh." That's terrific, seems we're all in the same mind. We have now achieved contact and we have connection."

Violetta and the Santos children stayed over in the Sanctuary for the final evening. Gabriel reflected on how friendships really flourish in adversity, and how comforting that was in the face of danger. Toby and Daisy both commented that they had so far enjoyed some terrific experiences and met some amazing people.

"Thank you for protecting us," said Toby to the trees on the way through the wood. "One important thing Daisy and I have learned is not to take good friends for granted, and to acknowledge any help we receive. This is something neither of us will ever forget."

Eddie Meadows was there waiting, right on time. He had brought a saloon car, a grey Humber with a walnut dashboard and leather seats, which was much more comfortable than the farm jeep. "Taxi for the seaside," he announced cheerfully. "It's only an hour away, so not much of a journey for you."

Daisy settled into the back seat next to Toby, hoping that an hour would soon pass, with less chance of them being discovered. The encounter with Dark Star at Broom Hill had been a shock but after ten minutes on the road, they were able to put it out of their minds. This time, there was definitely no threatening black Jaguar blocking the way.

16 DARKER SCHEMES

When Maxwell Delano was angry, the temperature dropped. Today, Red Tower's lounge with its plum settees was especially arctic. Irina Slack shivered as she walked through the door, bracing herself for the onslaught. Although life with Max certainly had its perks, his cold, angry moods were not on her list of favourite things. They always made her dream of sun-kissed beaches. Kicking off her high heels, she curled up on the squashy plum fabric of the nearest sofa, making herself as comfortable as possible.

"What's wrong with Shade?" Delano snapped, clenching his right fist. "He showed such a lot of promise, but so far the Order of Lumen has run rings around him. He's been, embarrassingly outwitted by a man who makes bath oil for a living. I could willingly kick that idiot Planks and his two stupid mates into the abyss and enjoy watching them scream." The black eyes became hellish slits, as the words shot into the freezing air like bullets.

Irina, wondering for a moment why Shade hadn't been included in the kicking into the abyss, put on her best, crisp manner. She knew from experience not to try to placate Max at moments such as this because it would make him angrier and she was already freezing. She visualized a roaring fire, which helped a little. This was one of the strategies she had devised over the years for her own comfort. Irina really thought that she was the only person who could deal with Max when he was annoyed, because she believed he trusted her. Her love of wealth and power and his understanding of Dark Star had bonded them together. Irina was waiting for instructions. "What do you intend to do?"

Max crossed his grey suited legs as he stared at the wall. He decided to fill Irina in on the events so far. "Greenway and the brats are gone. Hugo and the three stooges went to wait at Broom Hill station for them and they didn't turn up. Why not? Because they obviously had that figured out and had left by some other means. When we darken the Heart of Stars, that stupid woodland sanctuary is the first thing I intend to destroy. I'll break all its enchantments and the precious Order of Lumen will have nowhere to hide. I'll hunt down every single one of them until there's not a trace left, and the Lumerin will never enter this world again. I will rule here and everyone will do as I say. Dark Star is granting me the power.

Even though the temperature had just plummeted a few more degrees, Irina was practically ecstatic with the thought of all that destruction. "Of course, Max," Irina's manner displayed the malice of a coiled, hissing snake. "And I'll be right there beside you, as I always have been."

If Maxwell Delano had ever cared for anyone, it might certainly have been Irina because of her intense, though selfish, loyalty; but, sadly, he had undergone a gradual loss of feeling since he had begun to summon Dark Star. Now, there was only an iceberg in his heart, which nobody could melt, and like all icebergs, it was impossible to see how deep it went under the surface. Still, she was both trustworthy and efficient and those were qualities he needed, otherwise he would have thrown her out years ago, just like several others who had once been close to him. He didn't mention the secret deal he had sealed with Hugo, because he thought it was nothing to do with her. He had no intention of telling anyone and was sure that Shade would keep his mouth shut.

Deceiving Irina was of little importance to Max, because all he wanted now was to rule and dominate. He had become as lethal as a cold, steel sword. There was little humanity left and Dark Star was all that mattered. Irina would have scratched Shade's shifty eyes out if she had known what was really going on.

Ten years ago, Irina Slack had been a much warmer human being with the kind of energy and vitality that attracted friends. She had always been the most popular girl in any group, but now she kept people at a distance so that she could manipulate them whenever she chose.

The ice had crept in gradually as the Dark Star ceremonies slowly changed her, stealing the sunshine, to create an efficient machine with a cruel mind. Irina deluded herself that she was the only person Max cared about but in fact Max knew she was one of the only people left who could constantly stand his terrible presence without freezing up or screaming.

Max got to his feet and began pacing about because movement helped him to think. Finally, after six lengths of the room, he spoke. "Phone Shade at his hotel and tell him not to bother with the next Order of Lumen destination. I'll post a lookout there so we know when Greenway and the two kids arrive, and when they depart. Tell him to go straight to Mornington, because that's where they'll be heading around the start of Treefall. There won't be any Sanctuary to shelter them in the city and the presence of prominent Dark Star followers will help our cause. Direct him to my house in Bellham. It has the right atmosphere for making plans and a basement apartment to accommodate Planks, Mackintosh and Scally."

Irina, glad to be active, uncurled, put her shoes on and began to make her way to the phone in the study next door. Delano called her back with a second instruction, which awakened a little feeling of pleasure in her previously hardened heart.

"Now, is a good time for you to take the train down to Mornington, where you can keep an eye on Shade and the boys, as well as employing your skills to organize a successful kidnap and the theft of at least a couple of those stones the Order of Lumen have stashed somewhere. I'm putting you in charge now so make sure I'm not disappointed Irina – There can't be any more mess ups."

"Seriously Max, when have I ever messed up?"

Irina liked nothing better than being in charge, and apart from that, she quite fancied a break from Red Tower's cold rooms. She loved the sophistication and grandeur of Mornington. It was just her sort of place. She began to plan an itinerary; shopping, a day in a nice warm spa, lunch at Banbridge's with her sister, Belladonna, perhaps a new Ganelle suit, a hairdo and manicure at Jerome's and definitely a new pair of black patent stilettos… it was perfect.

Her eyes glowed with satisfaction as she sat at the desk, almost purring. In her imagination, she began pulling rank on Hugo, ordering him to do whatever she said. What choice would he have? She was, after all, second in command so she could do what she wanted. And then, of course, there was also the fun of getting rid of at least one of those pathetic prophecy brats.

* * * *

Hugo Shade was worried for the first time since his departure from Robinswood. As he told the others about Maxwell Delano's plans, Sid Planks' greasy face became ashen.

"Mr. Delano must be well mad about everything," he whined, "otherwise, why's Irina Slack joining in? She's very important you know."

"Yeah Hugo!" Jack's eyes narrowed dangerously. "You're obviously not making much of an impression are you?"

"Shut up, Scally you weasel," Shade spat. "If I'm in trouble, so are you. Or have you forgotten that we're all in this together?"

"Of course we haven't forgotten," chimed in Barry, "but it's just that you're in charge… see what I mean?"

Shade stormed off in a temper. A little fear was winding its way into his guts and he didn't want the others to notice his discomfort.

Sid Planks looked positively dejected. "You two haven't met Delano," he blurted. "We don't want to fall foul of him, believe me, and I, for one, would like to live to enjoy some fun with the money when all this is over." He desperately hoped that it would be over in his favour, though some uncertainty had begun to tug at the corners of his mind.

An hour later, Hugo Shade returned to the hotel, calm and focused. He had filled the Jag with petrol so that they could leave for the capital early tomorrow. He was now looking forward to staying at Max's place in Mornington and there would be a few of days of very welcome breathing space before Irina Slack took over. As real activities were not expected to begin until after the start of Treefall, Hugo intended to snatch as much time for himself as he could to go shopping in all the best stores.

17 SUNSHINE

Even though Daisy and Toby were both jumpy, an hour in the car soon passed. Gabriel, still and solid as a mountain, kept a keen eye out for signs of the enemy vehicle, whilst chatting about this and that in an attempt to keep the atmosphere light. Of course, none of them knew that Delano had told Shade to bypass this destination and head straight for Mornington. When they reached the coast road and the ocean came into view, Toby and Daisy forgot all about the possible dangers, watching the seagulls float on rafts of air above them, calling to each other in rays of sunlight streaming like molten gold across the clear azure sky.

"It's time to chill. There'll be shells to collect." Daisy had returned to being a happy girl. "And pebbles to paint. Fab-ul-ous!"

"Why do people always want to collect pebbles?" Toby asked. "I do it every time and then all they do is block up my pockets and deposit bits of sand everywhere, until I remember to take them out and leave them on the nearest convenient windowsill."

Daisy was scornful. "No imagination… shells are for painting with lovely colours and for sticking onto things along with my designer pebbles, right? Don't be so boring. What's wrong with you?"

"Nothing at all." Toby suppressed a smirk. "Perhaps some of the shells might contain creatures I can at least have an intelligent conversation with. I've never talked to fishy things before. By the way, yeah, what in heaven's name is a designer pebble?"

Daisy stopped the conversation and glared at him. She had no further need for his approval. The sun and the sea would soon sort out his stress.

At that point, Eddie began to turn into a driveway, a long narrow road that snaked its way between tree-lined lawns towards an imposing grey stone building at the end.

Only Gabriel had noticed a blue car parked on the other side of the road a short distance from the entrance. He couldn't clearly make out the driver, but it looked like a bespectacled woman who appeared to be studying a map. An uncomfortable feeling in his stomach alerted him to a possible threat. Gabriel made a mental note to investigate.

They parked by the front entrance of a stately country house which Toby remarked had every appearance of a castle with its numerous turrets and towers. Whatever history this building had, it was now a good hotel, with all the benefits of both a country and seaside location. The sign outside read:

ALLEGRIA HOTEL

RECEPTION

Oriel Solana appeared in a pale yellow dress belted with silver leather. Its delicate tone blended well with the long, straight, honey blonde hair hanging like curtains over her shoulders. A silver and gold pendant fashioned in the shape of a sunburst glinted around her neck and a bright smile lit up her almost violet eyes. Daisy gazed at the jewellery in admiration.

"What a totally gorgeous necklace."

"Thank you, it has a quality which helps those who look at it rise above their worries. An Order of Lumen craftsman made it - someone you'll meet when you go on from here to our capital city Mornington."

Daisy thought that she would be happy to meet such an

artist, but still tensed at the mention of Mornington. A sense of foreboding rose up from nowhere, like a rain cloud moving across the sun. She shrugged it off, putting it down to imagination. She had not yet learned to fully trust her instincts.

In the hotel office, Oriel ordered fruit scones with strawberry jam and clotted cream from the kitchen before updating them on the latest news about Dark Star.

"Hugo Shade and three other men have been dispatched to Mornington to join up with some other key people. Although there's little danger here, I'm afraid the next leg of your journey might prove to be very difficult. Delano must think he has more chance of stopping you in the city because a lot of Dark Star personnel work there. However, our own people are more than a match for them and the Lumerin are always amazing in the way they help us."

"Has the blue Austin car on the road been checked out?" Gabriel hadn't forgotten.

"It has, but my manager, Joseph, could find no trace of it. We'll do a check three times every day just to make sure. Your arrival may have been noted."

Oriel and Gabriel looked serious as they pondered this development. The cousins, however, wanted to get away from all this danger talk because the prospect of time at the seaside seemed like a free trip to heaven, which did not include Hugo Shade or greasy Planks. If the freshly baked scones with jam and clotted cream were anything to go by, the meals would be yummy.

A suite of rooms had been reserved for them at the very top of the hotel. In addition to the three small, but very comfortable bedrooms, there was a lounge and a bathroom so sumptuous, it would have made Hugo Shade very jealous. Gabriel was gratified to find a good selection of his own products next to a pile of folded fluffy towels.

"Here you are Daisy, Greenway's best wild rose and lavender soaps bath oils and cologne." He smiled with pleasure as her proudly showed her the green glass bottles and beautifully packaged soaps. "Of, course, I make quite a few different ones – Violetta Santos likes this spring orchid scent whereas Oriel prefers our lilac products and here's a ginger and lime one which is suitable for Toby and myself. One day I might even make a new range called Daisy."

"Seriously? … I'd love that, but these are so absolutely lush Gabriel, I'll try them all." Daisy opened up each of the bottles in turn but couldn't make her mind up which she liked the most. It was a nice touch that made them feel right at home.

"I was wondering Gabriel, if everyone staying here belongs to the Order of Lumen?" asked Toby after he and Daisy had smelled all the Greenway bath products.

"Not everyone, but all the guests have been screened for their good intention. Anyone undesirable would be told that the hotel's fully booked. Oriel insists that Joseph, in his twenty years as Hotel Manager, has never made a mistake."

An array of pretty gardens behind the hotel, descended in fragrant terraces which stopped at the small flight of steps leading on to the beach. There was a swimming pool, tennis courts and secluded places to sit with spectacular views of the ocean. Toby had decided that, in spite of Maxwell Delano's attempts to spoil everything, a stay at the Allegria Hotel was definitely going to be better than a holiday in Brighton. The sound of the seagulls and the view from his room were a real pleasure, whatever happened later.

"I defy you, Maxwell Delano," he murmured to the sky outside his bedroom window. "I defy you because you're total garbage, so me, my cousin Daisy and Gabriel, right? We're going to sort you out big time."

Oriel, who had supplied Daisy with paints and brushes, displayed the painted shells and patterned stones in porcelain dishes around the dining room.

"These are brilliant, Daisy," she said. "I think that part of your purpose in life is to create beauty as one means of healing souls. These bright things you've made have added something special to the atmosphere in here."

Daisy glowed in the warmth of the praise and felt very encouraged.

Toby, content with chatting to gulls most of the time, decided to take a swim in the sea instead of the pool one day in order to realize his ambition of trying to converse with fish. The attempt to get into deep water, however, was short lived because Gabriel wasn't happy.

"Get yourself back on this beach now Toby! Do you hear me! I've more than enough problems with Hugo Shade and Delano without adding the risk of you being swept away." Toby sulked and argued, but eventually did as he was told,

"You're overreacting Gabriel, give me a break!"

"Don't be such a dork," Daisy stuck up for Gabriel, "you've been weird since we got here. It's a lot of responsibility for Gabriel you know. We should think things through carefully. After all, we know nothing about the currents or tides here. It's common sense."

Toby came round and went back to the seagulls, marvelling at this strange development of Daisy talking about common sense. "Must be magic from Ynys Arian," he reasoned. "It's certainly unusual." The fact was, the more Toby's talent developed, the more sensitive he was becoming. He often found himself easily drained and irritated these days and it worried him so he mentioned it to Gabriel when they were alone.

"Don't fret Toby, it's a side effect of your communication ability. You must accept it and remember that we accept YOU whatever. Your gift has been so helpful on this trip and trust me, it will settle down, as you gain more understanding of it. In the meantime, this might help." Gabriel handed him a small blue bottle labelled Cloak of Flowers. "Take three drops every morning, it will help you to block out most of the rubbish, though I'm afraid not the full power of Dark Star, that's something you will eventually have to deal with."

"Thanks Gabriel, you always know what to do."

"Talk to me whenever you want and if necessary we'll phone

Dion because his gift is similar to yours. The other person who might be useful is, of course, your cousin with her colours. Why not go and ask her?" All of a sudden, Toby experienced a powerful sense of belonging as he set off to find Daisy; he had finally felt the connection and he knew that he wasn't alone.

The Lantern Ceremonies at Allegria were always held in a walled garden, which was locked to all guests who were not of the Order of Lumen. Daisy wondered whether the other people could see the light coming up over the wall and hear the singing.

"No," said Oriel, "we've created a sort of invisible bubble to keep the sights and sounds to ourselves. However, they do feel the presence of the Lumerin and, because it gives them such an air of wellbeing, they come back here year after year. One day, they'll become so receptive that they'll find the Order of Lumen. It is a natural process, like evolution, which happens without them trying to look for us. Of course, some people do look for us and do, indeed, find us when they're ready to know."

"Wicked," said Toby. "It just seeps into you and one day you know. That's so clever."

As Toby and Daisy were now participating fully in the ceremonies, they began to have a sense that there were only a few days left at the seaside hotel. The evenings were cooler and some of the foliage had begun to look dry and brown around the edges. The harvest had been gathered and the new season of Treefall was almost upon them.

On the morning of the eighty-eighth day of Greening, at breakfast, Daisy suddenly remembered the reason for staying there.

"What about the fourth stone?" she asked Gabriel at breakfast.

"It will be given today," he replied, "and, in fact, we're going to the walled garden as soon as you're ready."

The garden had quite a different appearance in the daytime; there was a rowan tree, lush with scarlet berries and fuchsia bushes hung with profusions of red and pink flowers. The borders and beds were resplendent rainbows of marguerites, asters, dahlias, geraniums and nasturtiums. Clematis and ivy trailed down the weathered stone of the sturdy wall behind the lantern plinth. At the centre of the garden, in a mosaic tiled circle, stood a well, protected by a bronze grid in the shape of a sunburst. The surface of the water sparkled as the sunlight danced upon it, revealing luminous green lichen and moss growing around its interior walls.

"Here's my well," said Oriel. "The sunlight gives the water a particular quality. It increases energy and promotes a positive outlook."

"Just the final ingredient I need for a special potion that the Lumerin instructed me to make." Gabriel looked at her knowingly.

"I'll give you as much as you need right now, and there'll always be more," replied Oriel, reaching through the sunburst grid to dislodge a loose stone in the interior wall of the well. Removing yet another small, leather pouch from the cavity, she handed it to Daisy. The jewel inside was a soft, clear yellow, like sunshine. The children both felt like laughing though they had no idea why.

"The Stone of Happiness."

Daisy placed it carefully into her belt bag, becoming the guardian of two jewels instead of one.

That night, Gabriel was given a small bottle of water so that he could complete the Lumerin's instructions for a potion that was already partially made.

"I suppose you'll know exactly when to use that potion," said Toby.

"Of course," Gabriel replied. "Isn't it always obvious?"

Before Ynys Arian, Toby would definitely have answered, "No!" to that question, but of late his senses had become more refined. An inner knowing was developing, an instinct which prompted the right course of action without him spending too much time thinking. He now understood that he had been headstrong and foolish about the fish, and was glad he had listened to Daisy's newly found common sense. Gabriel's more experienced instincts might well have been right. Although he was still a novice in the Order of Lumen, Toby was keen to learn as much as he could. It all felt very natural and right like he was remembering something important he'd known once before and then forgotten, but then didn't that happen all the time in Lumenor?

18 MORNINGTON

As Oriel's Mini pulled out of the hotel drive on the afternoon of the second day of Treefall, none of the passengers noticed the tweed-suited, bespectacled, middle-aged woman walking her Alsatian dog. Maybe it was because she looked so ordinary or maybe they were all too preoccupied thinking about their journey to Mornington. Certainly, during lunch, both Daisy and Toby had been going through a mixture of excitement and fear, which had lessened their appetites.

As soon as she spotted the white Mini on the main road, the woman with the dog headed off in the opposite direction towards the phone box, two hundred yards up the hill. Only Gabriel caught a glimpse of her from the corner of his eye, but Oriel drove away too quickly for him to dwell on what he had seen.

The nights were beginning to draw in with the change of season and the sun would already be setting when their late afternoon train arrived in Mornington at seven-thirty.

"So far, so good," Gabriel ushered Toby and Daisy on to the platform. There was no sign of the enemy and he had no wrenching feelings of danger in his gut. Five minutes later, they were on the train, in a compartment Oriel had reserved in advance. Daisy hastened to close the door as Toby pulled down the blinds.

"When we arrive in Mornington, we must stay close together," said Gabriel. "There's a substantial Dark Star presence in the capital and Hugo Shade's already lurking there somewhere, waiting for us."

The thought of people lurking in unknown places made Daisy tremble and the sudden, unexpected memory of Shade finding them at Oaklands did little to comfort her.

"What's the plan for when we get off the train, Gabriel?" she asked.

"We should all hold hands so that we don't become separated, then make our way, as quickly as possible, to the café up by Platform 14. It's very close to the taxi rank and Michael Dory will be waiting for us. Put your mind on Ynys Arian or any of our Order of Lumen friends, and try to get some rest if you can."

For some reason, Daisy decided to think about Rio the Unicorn and with that image lodged firmly in her mind, she fell into a shallow, fitful slumber until the train began to slow down.

"Wake up Daisy." Toby gave his cousin a gentle shake. "We're here."

As the train came to a halt, a large sign announced that they had arrived at Mornington Central.

Gabriel felt no alarm bells ringing when they alighted on Platform 3 into a crowd of passengers heading for the exit. Grabbing Toby and Daisy by the hand, he set off at considerable speed, weaving his way through the bustling throng until he reached the barrier, where he handed the tickets to the station official, before rushing off again towards Platform 14 with the children in tow. The busy concourse echoed with the din of noisy commuters heading home after a hard day's work.

All of a sudden, Toby pulled the other two to the left to avoid a couple of men he had spied standing a few yards in front of them directly in their path. "Why don't I like those two people, Gabriel?" he asked with a sharp intake of breath.

"Because you have a sense that there's something wrong."

Gabriel skirted around to the right again, towards a newspaper stand. "I'm glad to see you using your survival instincts, it means you've learned something since that fish incident."

Toby, blushing at the memory of his silliness, took a furtive glance back, but the men had disappeared into the crowd.

"Evening Chronicle! Get yer Evening Chronicle!" The voice of the newspaper seller echoed around the concourse as they headed for the Caprice Café just behind him.

"What a relief!" Michael Dory left his chair in such a hurry that he almost knocked over his mug of tepid station tea. "I've been worried sick," he said, getting as close to Gabriel as he could so that he could lower his voice. "There's been a lot of Dark Star activity going on here. Apparently, Irina Slack arrived last month. They say that Delano is furious and that's why he's sent her. We're going by cab, and I've already lined up a trustworthy driver. Come on, let's hurry."

They stuck close to Michael as he hurried towards the exit. Two minutes later, they were jumping into a black cab and slamming the heavy door behind them.

"Back to your house in Queensdown is it Mr. Dory?" asked the driver.

"Yes, please, Nightingale Square, as quick as you can, but without taking an obvious route."

"Leave it to me, I know just what to do, and it won't cost you a penny extra."

"No problem." Michael sounded a little weary from the constant tension. "Just get us there."

It took less time than they expected because the endless traffic lights were mostly green in their favour. The cabby remarked how lucky they were, and how unusual this was. In just under twenty minutes, they were standing outside Michael's home, an imposing Regency town house situated on one side of a very pretty square. Michael's was the first house of an elegant terrace of ten dwellings.

Although Gabriel carried out a careful scan of the street

before going inside, there was no way he could have seen the watching eyes behind the telescope in the attic of an equally elegant house on the opposite side of Nightingale Square. Michael had no idea that a high ranking Dark Star called Justin Feral, having persuaded its owner to rent it to him for an enormous fee, had moved in two days ago with his girlfriend, Belladonna Slack, Irina's younger sister.

Michael's sitting room was comfortable, though a little old fashioned. Well-stocked book- cases lined one wall and the old leather settees looked as if they had been there for a century. A welcoming fire crackled in the grate beneath a white marble fire surround. The visitors sat down whilst their host closed the heavy, brocade curtains, and switched on the stained glass Tiffany lamps.

"I design and create jewellery in silver and gold," Michael told Toby and Daisy, "each piece is inlaid with precious or semi-precious stones for a clientele who want something original. The things I make for members of the Order of Lumen are magical objects, all with a good purpose and empowered by the Lumerin - but of course you have already seen Oriel's sunburst necklace?"

"Yes and it was beautiful." Daisy was full of praise.

"It's been very easy to hide what you're here to collect," he remarked. "It's just with the other stuff in my safe. I could even put it on display and nobody would know that it came from the harp."

Michael's blue eyes were like deep pools amid the laughter lines in his kind, but confident, face. His dark blond hair, cut short for easy grooming, was as unobtrusive as his beige slacks and blue cotton shirt. The pallor of his skin suggested that he had spent most of the warm days indoors working.

In fact, Michael Dory, who was so passionate about his art, was no lover of hot weather, preferring to work all day and sit in the back garden of an evening with a glass of decent wine and a good book, or a couple of friends to talk to. There was no Mrs. Dory at the moment, but he did have an amazing tabby cat called Moses to keep him company. The cat made a beeline for Toby, who wasted no time befriending him.

After a satisfying dinner of hot chicken casserole with dumplings, Michael led the way to his basement workshop where a tall, black safe had been installed against the far wall. The workshop was a large room extending all the way to the back of the building, with a heavy door, which looked out of place in the party wall. Because it was an unusual feature and Daisy was nosy, she couldn't resist trying to open it.

"It's always locked. I keep the key here," said Michael, moving over to a chunky oak desk where he showed them all how to click open a small, secret compartment.

"Every house in this row belongs to members of the Order of Lumen. You can walk right to the end of the terrace through the basements, and this little key fits all the doors. I'm telling you this in case you ever need a quick escape. The garden at the rear of No. 10 has direct access into the side street."

"Wow! Now that's seriously awesome!" Toby loved stories about secret passages and hidey-holes in old manor houses and castles. "I'm really impressed, but I hope the Dark Stars don't know about it."

"Unlikely." Michael's certainty was comforting. "They're probably aware of me. Irina Slack, Hugo Shade and some other heavies are staying at Delano's house in Bellham, about four miles away. Slack's been sent because nasty old Max isn't too happy about the way things have been organized. There are also other Dark Star Elite here in this city, Irina Slack's younger sister, Belladonna, and a little creep called Justin Feral, to name just two. Delano's much more dangerous now and Irina Slack's a very nasty individual in high heels. I hear that Feral's getting into politics, so it's only a matter of time before the government's compromised."

"This place has a government?" Daisy looked shocked "Lumenor's full of surprises."

"Well, of course it does," replied Gabriel. "They deal with the day-to-day running of things. The Prime Minister knows a couple of people in the Order of Lumen, but he thinks they're businessmen. Of course, he hasn't the slightest idea who they really are. As you've likely been told, most people nowadays think we're a fairy tale, but once the jewels are returned and the harp's restored, then our influence will increase over a few generations, until we're back in everyday reality. It will be a wonderful world again for everyone, when the Lumerin become part of their lives."

Michael dialled the combination into his safe, pulled open the heavy door, and withdrew the customary leather pouch.

"This is the Stone of Love and Kindness," he said, tipping it into Toby's hand. Daisy loved the colour, which was the palest pink, soft and delicate like rose petals. Toby thought that he could smell flowers, but as a glance around failed to reveal a single vase so he could only assume that incredibly, the scent was coming from the jewel.

"It's best that you have the stone now," Michael added, "just in case. You never know with Dark Star."

Toby placed it gently into his belt bag, thinking that it would merit closer examination later.

"Right," said Gabriel, taking charge. "It's time for you two to get some sleep, and I hope you have enough energy left to climb up to the second floor."

Neither of them argued. After such a tense day, they were very grateful to be shown to their rooms, where they slept soundly until morning.

With Toby and Daisy safely tucked up under their blue and white blankets, Gabriel and Michael, who had known each other for most their lives, lounged on the old leather sofas downstairs, talking into the early hours, about Order of Lumen concerns, old friends, past times and future plans.

19 INTRUDERS

Next morning, just after sunrise, the milkman made his regular delivery of two bottles to No. 1 Nightingale Square. Always an early riser, Michael Dory greeted him on the doorstep, picked up the milk for breakfast and returned to the kitchen with it. Half an hour later the paperboy arrived and pushed the Mornington Daily News through the letterbox.

The first birdsong rose from the foliage in the square garden as a lone, urban fox made its crafty way home after a night's foraging. Belladonna Slack, unrecognizable, and undercover in spectacles and a headscarf, strolled along the pavement on her daily spying mission to pass on snippets of information to her sister Irina, who was busy in Bellham making plans to foil the Order of Lumen. It was a morning like any other, full of familiar, ordinary events, which would continue to repeat themselves over the following fourteen days.

After considering the news she had received from Belladonna's morning walks and Justin Feral's telescope sessions, Irina decided that it was time to act. It was time to send Hugo Shade, Planks, Mackintosh and Scally to stay in Nightingale Square. She would certainly be very glad to be rid of them, because Hugo's habit of constantly challenging her had become very annoying. She wasn't used to being questioned by anyone other than Max and the strong scent of Hugo's cologne was beginning to grate. That sickly, sophisticated smell always made her want to slap his face. She had begun to feel a growing resentment about the way Max always excused Shade's failures. Delano's attitude to such obvious bungling had annoyed Irina and caused a tinge of jealousy, thus adding fuel to her increasing dislike of the man.

Knowing how much Hugo loved his own company, Irina enjoyed ordering him to pack his bags and move into Nightingale Square to share the attic rooms with the other three fools. "Don't show Shade any favours, except for putting him in charge of the telescope surveillance from the top floor." She told Justin and Belladonna, "He should to be kept in his place at all times, and in my eyes, that place is somewhere near the bottom of the ladder only one up from revolting Planks."

A triumphant smile spread across Irina's red painted lips as she contemplated how much humiliation he might get from that. Irina always liked everyone in their place, with her and Max right at the top. Even her own sister, Belladonna, would always be less important in her eyes, and Shade was nobody.

On arrival at No. 28 Nightingale Square, Hugo Shade had a face like thunder. Justin faked an apology, "I'm sorry, old man, but we're using all the rooms on the first floor and the basement's storage space." Reminiscent of a small, brown ferret with a moustache, he delivered the bad news with an annoying smirk.

Hugo's expression became more guarded as he took on board the slight. Knowing that Justin was lying only increased his anger with Irina. He now hated her as much as Jack Scally hated him, for whilst the Order of Lumen had the ability to overcome their differences and cooperate for the common good, the destructive, critical nature of Dark Star always caused discord.

Making his way upstairs, Hugo congratulated himself. He had a secret that would shock Irina Slack right down to her silly, stiletto heels. In a private meeting with Delano three days before leaving Robinswood, he had received the key to a house situated on the north coast, a house off the beaten track, with a secret space under the floorboards in the back bedroom. Remembering Max's exact words filled him to the brim with triumph and satisfaction.

"The house has been put in trust for you, Hugo," Maxwell Delano had said. "In the unlikely event that I meet my destruction, I've made duplicates of all my Dark Star research, complete with incantations and maps. There's also a very substantial sum of money in cash and a bank- book showing a further amount I've lodged for you in a deposit account to meet your immediate needs. I've attached the name and address of a suitable lawyer to the deeds of properties and details of other business interests and investments I intend to leave to you should anything go wrong."

"I'm sure nothing will go wrong, but what about Irina Max?"

"Irina's only into all of this for what she can get. I know that and so does she. You, on the other hand, have my passion for Dark Star itself, which is why you are considered to be the most suitable heir. If all goes according to plan, which I hope it will, then you will be handsomely rewarded and become Dark Star's second in command."

"I don't know what to say Max." Hugo remembered his response to Delano's high opinion of him - how knocked out he had been by the unexpected amazing news.

"You're so like me, Hugo, that you are the obvious choice. I'm charging you, in the event of any mishap that you will go into hiding until the time is right to carry on my great purpose of ensuring that Dark Star rules this world. There's nothing more important or glorious. This charge to you is part of the instruction I have myself received. What do you say now, Hugo? Shall we drink to that?"

"Absolutely delighted." Hugo Shade had drained his glass, accepting Delano's offer to become his heir without the slightest hesitation, because Dark Star was the only thing he really loved in the whole world. Today, almost two seasons later, wrapped up warmly in his feelings of great pride, he was in no doubt whatsoever that he could afford to wait to have his revenge on Irina. The idea of that felt sweet.

In the attic, Shade claimed the telescope room for his own use and began his duties of watching the house on the other side of the square with a mocking obedience.

The milkman always began his round by delivering to the houses opposite Michael's, so on the morning of the seventeenth day of Treefall he walked up to No. 28 with the bottles clinking in his metal basket. As he deposited them on the step, the door opened to reveal Sid, Jack and Barry. Whilst Sid held the terrified man by pinning back his arms, Barry closed the door and Jack put a pad soaked with a knock out potion over his face, sending him into a drugged sleep. After that, it was easy to strip the unfortunate victim of his white coat and cap.

Looking every bit the milkman in his stolen clothes, Jack Scally nipped out to the float to continue the milk deliveries, while Hugo came down from the attic to usher Sid and Barry into Justin's car, which he then drove into the narrow street down the side of Michael's house. Belladonna Slack and Justin Feral remained indoors, taking turns to watch the show through the telescope.

As the sun rose over Nightingale Square, illuminating the morning dew on the spiders' webs, everyone was in place. Pulling his cap well down on his forehead, Jack Scally approached the door of No. 1 where Michael opened up as he arrived on the step.

Keeping his head down, Jack handed over the bottles to make sure that Michael's hands would not be free to fight back. He then grabbed him by the throat, pushing him backwards into the house. The knock out potion went swiftly over his face and all struggle stopped. Everything happened so fast that poor Michael had no time to cry out when Sid and Barry, sneaked round the corner and charged into the building. The only warning Gabriel got was the sound of the breaking glass as the milk bottles fell and smashed on the hard tiled floor in the hall.

All three intruders crashed into the kitchen before he could move.

Daisy screamed as she dropped the cereal box, scattering a mess of cornflakes everywhere. She made a desperate bolt for the back door, but Jack Scally captured her before she could get outside, pushing her roughly against the wall whilst Planks and Mackintosh went for Gabriel, who, though he fought like a hero, was thrown to the ground and knocked out amidst the crunching pile of cornflakes. Daisy was already bound and gagged when Hugo Shade stormed into the kitchen.

"Where's the other one?" he demanded. "Go and look for him, Mackintosh you ape!"

When the commotion started, Toby, who had been relaxing in the front room talking to Moses the cat, only had enough time to hide in the narrow space between one of the settees and the window. Crouching still as a statue, he tried to breathe quietly as Barry Mackintosh lumbered through the door with a stupid grin on his face.

Toby could feel the presence of his pursuer like an animal senses a predator. Moses the cat sat on the carpet by the door, hissing at the clumsy intruder. It was, indeed, fortunate that Barry had been chosen to search for Toby, because being the most stupid of the trio, he was far too lazy to look behind furniture.

"Nobody in here," Toby heard him say as he moved on to the dining room next door.

"Then go and look upstairs, you clown." Shade's manner was rude and impatient. "Sid and I are taking the girl to the car. Get yourself outside, Scally, and check the garden."

After hearing Barry lumbering up the steps to the first floor, Toby left his hiding place and chanced a cautious peek towards the kitchen. He couldn't see or hear anyone, so he decided that the other intruders must have made an exit through the back door. There was no sign of Gabriel, but his stomach lurched as he saw Michael lying on the floor amidst the broken glass and white pools of spilled milk. As there was no blood, and Michael was still breathing, he made a snap decision to go for help.

Quiet as a mouse, Toby nipped down the staircase from the hall to the basement where he entered the workshop and retrieved the key from its secret hiding place. There were movements and voices upstairs again as he opened up the exit in the party wall, to slip through into the cellar of the house next door, and then on along the row.

When he let himself into No. 3, Toby was immediately startled by the unexpected presence of a brown skinned man waiting for him in the centre of the basement room. He froze, unsure what to do next.

"It's okay," the stranger assured him. "I'm Krishan Sharma, of the Order of Lumen, I live four doors down. We know that Dark Star's here. Tell me what has happened. I am going to help you."

Trusting his instincts, Toby gave a hurried, but precise, account of the events at Michael's house, though he was shaking with fright and worry about his cousin and friends.

Go on to No. 7," Krishan instructed him. "My wife, Kavita will be waiting for you. I will check out Michael's and join you later."

"Please be careful." Toby 's voice was strained and anxious. "There are four men and I know that at least one of my companions has been attacked and injured."

By the time Krishan arrived at Michael's, there was no sign of the intruders. Michael was beginning to wake up and Gabriel having regained consciousness was sitting upright against the kitchen wall holding his aching head. Though Krishan called and searched throughout the entire house and garden, he could not find her. Daisy was missing.

"I need a bottle of Rapid Healer, Krish," Gabriel moaned. "It's in my rucksack upstairs."

The potion soon put Gabriel and Michael back on their feet, but only to hear the terrible news of Daisy's capture.

"No way…" wailed Gabriel in angry despair, holding his head again.

"And Toby?" asked Michael, hardly daring to hope.

"Toby's safe at my place with Kavita." Krishan's good news was, indeed, welcome. "Now, we must also go there, so let us lock up the doors and get all your things. Kavita and I will come back later to clean up this ghastly mess."

Retrieving the children's rucksacks from their rooms, Gabriel suddenly thought about Daisy's harp stones, but then remembered that she had been wearing the new pyjamas and dressing gown that Michael's cleaner, Mary, had brought. The belt bag containing the two jewels was under her pillow, where she put it every night. Barry Mackintosh had been too stupid to search for it and Toby, already dressed, had been wearing his. It was some small relief in the face of a grand disaster.

Sometime after the event, a very groggy milkman woke up under a tree in the garden at the centre of Nightingale Square, with his cap and coat on the ground beside him. He remembered nothing and hadn't the slightest idea how he came to be lying on the grass in that garden. When at last he found his float, he was surprised to discover that most of his milk had in fact been delivered. It was one of those mysteries that would never be solved.

20 THE FOX

A quiet, graceful woman in a lilac sari, Kavita Sharma had quickly busied herself with the task of looking after Toby and was just passing him a clean cotton hanky when Gabriel and Michael arrived. Toby's distress at the loss of his cousin Daisy had finally got the better of him, causing the tears to fall freely.

"Look, he's just a boy." Kavita, was sympathetic. "He's so young to be tolerating these terrible circumstances, prophecy or not. I wouldn't have wanted my own children to go through this experience at such a young age."

"Nor would anybody," agreed Gabriel in a gentle tone, his eyes misting over as he thought about Daisy. "But, then, these are difficult times, Kavita, when all civilized life is threatened. These children are our only hope of saving Lumenor and I've been foolish enough to lose Daisy."

He pulled the box of special Lumerin remedies from his rucksack, and began searching for one to help Toby. "This should do," he said, unscrewing the dropper of something called Shock Buster. Toby accepted the drops without comment, becoming calmer and regaining his colour in seconds.

"What do we do now? What'll happen to Daisy? What if they kill her to stop the prophecy from working?"

Kavita closed her eyes in concentration. "They won't kill her. I'll make a few enquiries and we'll talk to the Lumerin. Right now, my extra senses tell me Daisy's unharmed and will be safe for at least three days. If we keep her in a happy place in our minds and hearts, then I think this will afford her some protection."

"I'll try." Toby made an attempt to sound convincing. Grateful to Kavita's extra senses, he began to picture Daisy singing the Lumerinda in the Sanctuary, which he thought would provide two protective images. Gradually, the knot in his stomach began to unwind, though the day seemed long and staying on top required a continuous mental effort.

At twilight, a sombre party of five conducted a lantern ceremony in the Sharmas' conservatory, with only the top windows open to let in the Lumerin. The light was like pale rainbows in silver white and the voices of the Lumerin comforting and sweet.

It was now understood that Daisy had been taken to Delano's house in Bellham, but that Irina intended to move her to a different location after midnight. Toby was instructed to look out for a visitor who would bring the exact details as soon as Dark Star's plans were known.

"Animals, birds... creepy crawlies?" reasoned Gabriel. "Must be something like that, if the information's coming to Toby."

Toby, however, couldn't see how that was going to work, when he was stuck in the middle of a city with no possibility of going out. It was such a depressing prospect that he forced himself to pursue happy thoughts of Daisy again. "I have to trust," he reminded himself. "The Lumerin have never let us down."

The day's events had been so exhausting that Toby decided to go to bed early. In spite of mental fatigue, the tension in his muscles kept him awake for a full hour. Eventually, he fell into a string of confused dreams, which wound up in a green meadow where a unicorn grazed in a haze of golden sparks.

"Is that you, Rio?" he asked moving closer.

"Wake up, Toby," came the reply like persistent silver bells. "Wake up! Wake up and go to the window!"

The image faded abruptly as Toby awoke with a jolt. Although the room was dark, his head was full of light as if someone had flicked a switch in his brain. The alarm clock on the bedside table showed a quarter to one. From his first floor room at the back of the house with a clear view across the garden, Toby spied an eagle owl folding her wings in the tree on the lawn.

"Two Hoots!" exclaimed Toby, surprised.

"No, I am not," replied the owl, "but I do know him well."

"He told me to keep an eye on Daisy and I didn't," admitted Toby, downcast.

"It is not your fault," insisted the owl. "This Dark Star is more foul and powerful than you can possibly imagine. So far, in spite of your inexperience with such matters, you have done remarkably well and believe me when I say this - all is definitely not lost."

Toby rallied a little from the owl's encouragement. "What can you tell me?" he asked eagerly.

"Plenty." The owl's eyes rolled like spinning amber coals. "The girl was moved from Delano's house just after midnight. She has been taken to a new destination by the river. It is about two miles as the owl flies - a row of detached houses on the waterfront, which are all different colours. The grey one at the end of the road has a boathouse and a jetty at the rear, where Dark Star has moored a new motorboat. The girl has been imprisoned in the boathouse and I am happy to report that she is very much alive."

"Thanks so much!" Toby almost collapsed with relief. He hoped desperately that Irina Slack hadn't injured Daisy.

"Do not mention it," replied the owl unfurling her tawny wings and hooting three times before rising into the air.

"Three Hoots!" Toby was shouting and running as fast as he could towards Gabriel's room. He didn't care what time it was. It was just time to get up.

The commotion not only awakened Gabriel but both Sharmas and even Michael, who had claimed lodgings for the night on the floor above. Wearing their dressing gowns and slippers, they congregated on the first floor landing to see what all the noise was about.

"It's one o'clock in the morning" ... moaned Michael, rubbing the sleep from his eyes.

Once Toby had explained about his encounter with the owl, Krishan decided to make a phone call and then meet up with the others in the conservatory.

"We have a friend," he explained, "someone I think will be able to help us, even at this early hour and as luck would have it, she lives at No. 4."

"Seren!" Michael smiled broadly. "Of course."

Toby was intrigued, but did not delay the call by asking questions.

Krishan soon returned with good news. "She's been out already and has just come home, but she'll be here in fifteen minutes."

Seren Shore, petite and auburn haired looked neat and sprightly in her tartan trousers and bottle green sweater. She breezed into the conservatory with all the grace of a ballet dancer, and after hugging everyone, introduced herself to Toby.

"Are you familiar with a row of coloured houses fronting the river about two miles from here?" inquired Gabriel. "We believe that Daisy's in the boathouse of the grey one."

"It's a minor Dark Star house which is often empty because the owner works away a lot. I'd be happy to go and check it out, have a nose around and try to find out who's there."

"Can I come with you?" asked Toby. "I need to be occupied. I need to be looking for my cousin."

"Patience, Toby," came Krishan's reply. "I'm afraid that's not possible. You'll understand in a minute."

"I'll be back before dawn," Seren assured them. "Try not to worry, Toby. I'm a good little spy with considerable experience."

What happened next was a total shock to Toby. As Seren made her way to the outer door of the conservatory, she seemed to be floating in a mist, her form becoming less and less distinct until she finally vanished in a swirl of light . There was no further trace of any human being, only a splendid fox with an auburn coat remained in the open doorway, her nose twitching as she looked at Toby through sharp brown eyes.

"Awesome!" Toby could scarcely believe the sudden unexpected transformation.

"This belongs to Daisy." Gabriel held out the knitted jacket so that Seren could pick up the scent.

Although the fox had no human voice with which to speak, she echoed loudly through Toby's mind as she padded out into the garden, making her stealthy way through the hedge into the familiar foxy trails she had travelled many times before.

"I'll find her, you can count on it." Toby could still hear her even though Seren was now out of sight.

"She's on her way now," said Kavita, "and all we can do is wait. We don't all need to stay up. You can certainly go to bed, Toby, if you want to, and I'll wake you when she comes back.

"I'm much too stressed to go to bed and I think that trying to sleep will be a waste of time." After a half-hearted attempt to persuade him, Gabriel, too weary to argue, gave in and let him stay up. Kavita brought tea and vegetable samosas, which distracted them for a while from the seriousness of their situation but even so, the wait was endless.

Before sunrise, the fox returned, trotting across the dark garden towards the conservatory. In another swirl of light, Seren Shore was back in human form.

"I could murder a cup of coffee... anything to eat? I didn't have time to hunt rabbits."

Toby grimaced at the thought of raw rabbit. Seren grinned, displaying her even, white teeth.

"I'm joking," she said, "but then again, if I had to stay in fox form for a long time, I might not have a choice."

"Tell us who was there." Gabriel was impatient. "Did you see any cars?"

Seren curled up in an armchair with the coffee and samosas

Krishan had given her

"Firstly, I think there were a few people at the house, because there were two smart looking cars in the drive. The boathouse has a locked door and only one tiny window. My creature instincts picked up a living scent, which matched the one on Daisy's jacket."

"Was one of the cars a black Jaguar?"

"Definitely! Anyway, standing out of sight but close to the French windows, I saw four people: Irina and Belladonna Slack, Justin Feral and Hugo Shade. It was a surprise that they were still up at such a late hour - but fortunate, because when I'm a fox, my hearing's so acute I can pick up conversation through glass. Irina announced her intention to interrogate Daisy about Order of Lumen arrangements. She was devising plans to make Daisy's life a misery before further instructions from Delano in two days' time and she was furious that Daisy didn't have any of the harp stones on her."

Gabriel was thoughtful. "It's a relief to hear that Daisy's safe until Delano says otherwise. We do at least have a chance now. Did you see Planks, Mackintosh and Scally?"

"No," she answered, "though I wouldn't recognize them, but as they're not important enough to have any part in the Dark Star's strategic planning, I think they'd probably gone to bed. I'm sure Daisy's in danger, and we must rescue her tonight, before Delano has any opportunity to give further orders."

"I'll kill them if they hurt her!" blurted out Toby, giving way to desperation in the wake of Seren's information.

Gabriel tried to soothe him. "Nobody's going to be hurt. We'll get her out tonight, as soon as it gets dark. Let's draw up a plan of action, call the people we need to help us, and then try to get some sleep, so that we have enough energy to cope with what might prove to be a very long and difficult night."

"My brother has a boat," said Krishan. "I'll go and call him right now."

21 THE BOATHOUSE

Remembering very little about the drive from Nightingale Square to Delano's house in a street called Bellham Park Drive, Daisy assumed that she must have passed out from the shock. Now she was waking from a bad dream about falling down a black hole into space, only to enter another very real nightmare, with the sneering face of Irina Slack glaring down at her as she opened her eyes. Daisy had been dumped on a chair in a sitting position.

The pain from her bound ankles and wrists brought her back to full consciousness. She took a deep breath as Irina untied the horrible scarf donated by Hugo Shade to serve as a gag. The nauseating smell of cologne on the silken fabric had made her want to retch.

"Well, now, the kid's awake!" Irina's voice sounded poisonous. "Where are the jewels you were carrying?"

"As you can see, I'm still in my pyjamas and dressing gown." Daisy screwed her face up and tried to sound sarcastic even though she was terrified by the hate she could feel oozing from Irina. "I don't have anywhere to keep any stones you total dope... Alright!"

"No matter," spat Irina. "We have you and the Order of Lumen don't. Without you, there's no prophecy and in any case, those seven minor stones are useless to your revolting pals without the Heart of Stars."

Daisy shivered, refusing to allow the mounting fear to overcome her. Letting the words of the Lumerinda flow through her mind made her feel braver and increased her determination to stand up to Irina. She was surprised by the strength of her own courage.

Hugo Shade, who was watching with interest, enjoyed seeing Irina on the verge of losing her cool, but then, remembering whose side he was on, he decided to intervene.

"A spell on her own without food or water will sort her out. Dump her upstairs, Scally! She'll have time to cool down before Irina questions her about the Order of Lumen and their pathetic plans. Make sure you put the gag back on. We don't want her waking the neighbours now, do we?" Jack never argued with Hugo when Irina was there.

By this time, Irina was seething, not just about Daisy, but also about Shade's interference. It was duly noted with a view to future vengeance. "Get her out of my sight," she ordered, resuming her position of control before making a grand exit like a nasty tornado.

Hoisting Daisy over his shoulder, Jack Scally transported her to a bedroom on the top floor, where he untied the biting cords and pushed her onto an uncomfortable couch. "You be good now!" he sneered before closing and locking the door behind him.

Sitting with her back against a wall, Daisy rubbed her hands and feet to increase the circulation before exploring her dreary prison. The room had a small bathroom and a dormer window, which refused to budge, however hard she pushed and the door was well and truly locked. It was useless to try to escape. She really had become a captive of Dark Star, and now she would have to deal with that.

The realization was shocking. For all her bravado, she knew she was no match for seven nasty adults, and began to wonder what her fate would be if nobody arrived to rescue her. What if they just left her to starve - or worse?

Daisy had started to lose herself as terror took hold and a creeping darkness began to engulf her mind. The room filled with whispering shadows, as a silent scream formed in her throat. The cold seeped into her bones and despair gradually tiptoed in like a thief stealing a lantern.

Just as she was about to slip into total panic, Daisy experienced a sudden image of golden sparks, and the comforting face of the unicorn, "Rio," she gasped, letting out a sigh of relief, " is that really you?"

"Stay with me, Daisy, do not get lost. I insist that you stay with me. I will always show you the way."

The shadows began to melt as light filled her head, prompting a further attempt at a silent chant of the Lumerinda.

With that, another very positive memory arrived - a memory of Oriel Solana, sitting in the garden of the Allegria Hotel. Though it was less than three weeks since the event, all that happiness had seemed a lifetime ago in this Dark Star hell. Oriel's words came back to her, reassuring and restoring.

"If you feel lost, you can always count on a unicorn, especially if you can call one by name." Oriel knew a great deal of unicorn lore having once studied it in depth.

"Rio, Rio," Daisy called silently, over and over until the daylight faded outside. Finally, she fell asleep until Jack Scally returned accompanied by Belladonna Slack. Although Belladonna bore quite a strong resemblance to Irina, she preferred to wear less makeup and casual clothes. Eleven years younger and less experienced than her sister, she had already learned to snap like a crocodile.

"Drink this!" Belladonna grudgingly handed Daisy a glass of milk. "Tie her up again, Scally, and don't forget the gag. We don't want any calls for help."

Daisy decided not to protest, even though Belladonna looked much less dangerous than Irina. She drank the milk warily, and only because her throat felt parched.

Once the cords were back in place, Jack Scally hoisted Daisy over his shoulder a second time, took her out into the night and pushed her on the back seat of the familiar black Jaguar. Sandwiched between Sid Planks and Barry Mackintosh, she was very uncomfortable and wanted to scream.

"Where are the others?" inquired Sid.

"They'll follow in Feral's car as soon as we've got the river house opened up and stashed the brat in the boat shed outside." Shade sounded bored.

The grubby mattress in the chilly boathouse looked less than inviting to Daisy, as Scally dumped her on it like a sack of rubbish. This time, he left without untying her. There was only a tatty satin eiderdown she could wriggle under to keep out the damp from the proximity of the river. They obviously did not want her to freeze to death before she had told them what they wanted to know. The thought offered precious little comfort. Daisy made another effort to focus on Rio, as well as repeating the words of the Lumerinda. Although sleep had seemed impossible, it did finally come, shutting out all the cold misery of this new dank prison.

Just after daylight, Irina and Belladonna Slack resumed their interrogation. Irina did the talking, whilst Belladonna watched and learned. Daisy, innocent, knew nothing about any plans, as Gabriel only received Lumerin instructions when the time was right. It had been a good precaution and as she had no idea at all of Toby's whereabouts there was no need to invent any convincing lies. She could only hope that he was safe somewhere with Gabriel.

Irina Slack paced up and down a lot, huffing, puffing and snapping, but Daisy could still tell her nothing.

"You're lying," insisted Irina, returning again and again to the same questions about the Order of Lumen and the harp stones.

Eventually, Daisy was given some stale bread and jam with disgusting tea. With little inclination to eat their foul stuff, instinct told her to keep up her strength and survive. In spite of her reluctance, she ate what she was given and didn't argue.

During the long day Irina and Belladonna returned to the boathouse twice, torturing her with more futile questions and insults, but there was never any information.

"Another night in the cold will sort her out," Irina decided. "And then, if she doesn't talk, I expect Max will want to get rid of her to foil the prophecy."

"Why not do that now and save ourselves some trouble?" suggested Belladonna, trying to sound clever.

"Because Max wants to locate the other seven stones." Irina replied. "They form a set with the big one we've already nabbed, the one he's going to corrupt with the incantation on The Eve of Threshold. If we don't mess them all up, the Order of Lumen might one day discover a way to recreate their precious Heart of Stars. Max will only get rid of her if and when he's absolutely certain that she doesn't know anything."

The merciless heels clattered across the concrete floor as Irina breezed away, followed by her sister. Left to her own company, Daisy could see through the tiny window that it was now almost dark outside. Lonely and frightened, she put her mind back on Rio and began to call his name until his face filled her imagination again. She had a strange notion that he winked at her before she dozed off.

Daisy awoke with a start. She could hear someone outside, someone who seemed to be having difficulty with the lock. Trembling with cold, she braced herself for yet another pointless interrogation. Finally the door was ajar, allowing a woman smaller than Irina to slip through the gap. Soon the painful bonds and Hugo Shade's foul gag were removed.

"I haven't the slightest idea who you are or how you got in but I'm mega pleased to see you." Daisy was so grateful to be free she was tearful.

"I'm a friend of Michael Dory. He makes exceptionally good skeleton keys as well as beautiful jewellery." Seren Shore helped her off the tatty mattress and held up the key on a ribbon. Daisy hung it around her neck without any idea that her rescuer had done exactly the same before changing into a fox.

"Give that key to Gabriel, you never know, it might come in useful later."

Together they crept out towards the unlit jetty where the Dark Star motorboat was moored. Another boat, its engine cut, had glided up beside it. Amrit Sharma climbed out to lift Daisy down to Gabriel before sneaking into the Dark Star craft, where he swiftly and skillfully disabled its engine. There was a swirl of light as Seren resumed her fox shape, padding across the grass to take up position closer to the house.

"They must have put something in their rancid tea or I'm going bonkers, Gabriel," whispered Daisy, sounding disturbed. "The woman who got me out just turned into a fox."

"Shush," he said, putting his finger to his lips. "She really did turn into a fox and I'll explain later."

"Time to go." Amrit had climbed back on board and was busy starting up the engine. Immediately the boat pulled away, the French windows burst open, spilling Hugo Shade, and Justin Feral on to the lawn. A shocked, angry Irina followed, pushing Belladonna out in front of her.

The garden was suddenly alive with foxes, as Sid Jack and Barry arrived, awakened by the commotion. There must have been twenty or more zigzagging everywhere, tripping and nipping legs. The Dark Stars toppled like skittles, attacked over and over as they tried to get up. It was the worst possible punishment for Irina and Justin, who loathed animals even more than Hugo did.

Eventually, Hugo Shade managed to clamber to his feet and tear towards the jetty, jumping into the boat with every intention of following Amrit. The engine wouldn't fire up. Looking first confused, and then desperate, he lost his temper, thumping the steering wheel until his fists hurt. Jumping out of the broken boat, he beat a hasty retreat through the red peril, towards the house, aiming hard kicks at the nipping mouths.

"Get in the cars," he commanded, trying to catch his breath. "Follow the river!"

Almost as if an invisible someone had called to them, the foxes promptly let go of their prey and disappeared into the undergrowth, leaving six dishevelled Dark Stars free to head for the front drive. Irina limped as one of the stiletto heels broke on her new, black patent shoes. Giving way to rage, she pulled them off and flung them in the privet hedge.

Hugo Shade cursed loudly when he discovered that his beloved Jag had two flat tyres, and Justin looked like he might cry when he saw that that the same had been done to his own motor. Nobody had noticed an old man with a walking stick and a dog strolling along the street just after sunset. Nobody saw him unsheathe the hidden spike at the end of his cane and stick it in the front wheels of both cars before continuing on his merry way home, happy to have been of service.

Pushing the engine to its limits, Amrit was mooring at his own house twenty minutes later. Gabriel kept chuckling to himself. "It's not only that we've got Daisy back," he chortled, "but also that I can't help thinking how hacked off Maxwell Delano is going to be. I sure wouldn't want to be Irina Slack right now!"

Toby was ecstatic to be reunited with Daisy, hugging her like she had been away for years. "I swear, Daise, that whatever you might do to annoy me that I'll never wish you back in Wales as long as I live."

"It's horrendous, Toby," she sobbed. "It's like the darkness creeps right into your bones and freezes you up from the inside."

"I'm sorry," he apologized. "I should have tried to fight them at Michael's."

"And then I would have lost both of you," Gabriel interrupted sternly. "Very bad idea, I think not!"

After a brief explanation to Daisy about Seren Shore and her shape-shifting abilities, Gabriel passed her the familiar rucksack so that she could go upstairs to wash and change.

Daisy was delighted to see that the bag of harp stones was there on the top, waiting for her like an old friend. She put on clothes that Morag had given her in the season of Floria because the temperatures were a little cool for shorts and sandals now. The new, black leather, buckled shoes and white ankle socks provided by Kavita were comfortable, and the memory of Morag pleasant as she hugged the warm hand-knitted jacket around her.

"Michael will be driving you," explained Amrit. "I'm lending him my new car."

Michael was more than a little pleased to be going with them. "A few days away at the school will do me good. There's something important I need to study."

No one had time to ask about that because Gabriel was in a hurry to be on the road. "We should go now. It's only a couple of hours' drive, but I'm anxious to get away before they regroup and start looking for us." Michael and his three passengers boarded Amrit's new Rover complete with sandwiches and flasks.

"Bit conspicuous, this car, Amrit," said Michael, "though exactly what you might expect for an Order of Lumen lawyer."

Amrit had chosen the car after a lot of test drives. "They won't be expecting conspicuous... anyway, it's the best I can do. I've only had this car for one season, so please try very hard not to damage it."

"Don't worry," Michael assured him, revving the engine with considerable pleasure at the thought of driving such a lovely machine. "I'll bring it back in mint condition. See you in about fourteen days."

Amrit waved wistfully as his new toy disappeared into the night. Daisy, tired and hungry, was already opening up her pack of sandwiches.

22 ADVANCED LUMERIN STUDIES

Comfortable and safe after her ordeal, Daisy had no trouble falling asleep in the back seat as they journeyed northeast, always on the lookout for Hugo Shade's Jaguar but eventually, after eleven o'clock, there was very little traffic. The major highways they had travelled on until now had been replaced by B class country roads and finally single tracks.

With the villages all behind them, the route meandered across empty moorland, populated only by sheep, a few trees and occasional rocky outcrops. It was too dark to get a glimpse of the sea to the east, as the track snaked around a hillside to a solid grey stone building at the summit. At the time of the dark moon, very little was visible, though the sound of the waves was unmistakable once they were out of the car.

"This is Falconhurst," Gabriel told his friends. "It's an Order of Lumen secret retreat and our school for advanced Lumerin studies, though you'll see no sign outside to advertise that."

"A school?" Toby was far too tired to cope with education.

"A school with a bit of a difference," chuckled Michael, approaching the impressive main entrance and ringing the bell. "Different, because there are no children here – well, that is, apart from you, of course."

Two people greeted them with so much enthusiasm that it would have been impossible not to feel welcome and at home.

"Come in, come in!" The tall cheerful woman had a deep cello voice. "I'm Raven Stone, Principal of Falconhurst, and this is Eli Stone," she said.

"Honoured," said the pleasant thin man who was even taller. "I've been studying my charts and waiting patiently for this day, and now at last here you are, exactly according to plan and bang on time too."

As if in agreement, the grandfather clock at the foot of the polished staircase chimed midnight. Eli Stone led the way to the single study bedrooms at the top of the second flight where the aged floorboards along the narrow corridor creaked loudly. Fresh towels and new pyjamas had been laid out on the purple candlewick bedspreads. Daisy fell on to her bed instantly, relieved to be safe and cared for once again.

Exhausted from the Mornington experience, the two young ones slept deeply and woke much later than usual. It was almost ten o'clock when Gabriel knocked on their doors to ask them if they would like to come down for a cooked breakfast of bacon, eggs and toast.

Although there had been a little early rain, the day was bright and breezy with fast moving clouds. The pewter grey ocean heaved and pounded against the cliffs, as the piercing noise of seabirds rose and fell with the high tide. This was a very different seascape to the gentle south coast. In its lonely wildness, it had a stark beauty all of its own.

It wasn't long before Toby and Daisy were bounding down the staircase, complaining that they were starving and looking for the kitchen. The joyful noise of children was so unusual in this remote house that it cheered Raven's heart to hear their lively voices.

"Did you say you're in charge here?" Daisy felt more alert than when she had first arrived.

"I am, indeed, the principal," Raven replied, "though I share the duties with my husband, Eli. He's a very accomplished astronomer and astrologer. You're welcome to go to the observatory to look through the telescope. I'm sure you'll learn something, and he'll be very pleased to show you the night sky."

"Looks like there's going to be some fun stuff here, then," Toby said. "Not like normal school at all."

"My own subject is hymns, chants and incantations," Raven explained, "although I have learned to work with the Lumerin in many different ways. As usual at this time of year we have very few adult students so I will have a measure of free time to devote to you."

Toby and Daisy had both warmed to Raven Stone because of her easy   personality. Lithe and strong as a lioness with ebony skin and closely cropped hair like grey wool, she looked stately but lively in her violet robe. Eli, though he had the same complexion and garment, seemed a little more guarded, polite in an old-fashioned sort of way. The mop of silvery dreadlocks combined with a pair of small round tortoiseshell specs, created an interesting if not slightly wacky appearance.

After breakfast, Gabriel showed them around the school. The library was divided into labelled sections. Toby read them out. "Lumerin Contact, Communication, Ancient Lumen, Incantations, Hymns and Chants, Lantern Studies, Unicorn Lore, Shape Shifters, Plants, Herbs and Trees, Empowerment of Objects…" He soon gave up because there were so many.

Next door, they discovered a separate records room with leather bound volumes containing the entire history of the Order of Lumen to date.

"One day, students will be able to read your story in this room," said Gabriel proudly. "Morag's begun working on it already."

"Fascinating," Toby replied. "It's got to be better here than Oxford."

In the days that followed, Raven taught Toby and Daisy a new chant – a song that the Lumerin had described as vital to their mission. She advised them to learn it, and learn it well. Gabriel had given them a few drops of Remember Me potion just to make sure that they forgot neither the words nor the tune.

"Why's it so important?" Toby was aware of the danger again.

"Have faith - the Lumerin reveal their reasons in their own time. You'll know when to sing it. It's called the Heartsong." It was certainly intriguing, though worrying at the same time, but they began to practice just as often as learning the Lumerinda in the Sanctuary.

Michael spent lot of time engaged in study, but joined them each day for dinner. One evening, Daisy looked up from her treacle sponge. "What have you been learning today, Michael?"

"I've been reading up on shape-shifting," he answered, keeping his eyes on his pudding bowl.

"Thinking of turning into something interesting then?" Gabriel's tone was teasing.

Toby tried to imagine what sort of creature Michael might become. "How about an eagle?" he suggested, trying to come up with something powerful and majestic for his friend.

"Or how about a wood louse?" joked Gabriel, poking fun again.

Michael refused to be goaded. "You can't just turn into things - it has to be in your background. No, I thought I'd like to understand a bit more about Seren, as she only lives three doors away."

"He's got that soppy look on his face," sniggered Daisy. "I think Michael's in love with Seren. What do you think, Gabriel?"

Michael smiled, trying not to be drawn in.

"You're right Daisy, it's been obvious for ages. Everybody knows."

"Like they know how soft you are on Sage Flowers?"

"We're both into plants - so what? We've a lot in common."

"Of course you do!" Michael's smile turned into a giant grin, but he soon became thoughtful again and finally wistful. "How can there possibly be any personal happiness until this mess is solved? We're not out of danger. You'll certainly find the sixth stone here, but there's still one more to collect, and then -

somehow - you have to persuade Maxwell Delano to part with the Heart of Stars, which he has stolen and wants to corrupt. I'm not even allowed to help you."

"It will be all right, my friend," Gabriel assured him, becoming serious. "It will be all right - you'll see, and next Threshold we'll have a great party with music and dancing."

"That's happy days then, and since you make jewellery, Michael, you'll be able design the most gorgeous, luscious ring in the whole of Lumenor for Seren." Daisy sighed and went all dewy eyed. She loved a wedding.

"Oh, boring!" Toby grimaced. "Why do you always think of such dopey things?"

Michael laughed as Daisy aimed a playful kick at her cousin. The mood had already lifted.

Keeping his promise to return Amrit's new car, Michael Dory left Falconhurst on a cloudy night seven days later. "I don't expect Dark Star to show any further interest in Nightingale Square, but, nevertheless, I do intend to be on my guard." Sorry to see their friend leave, Daisy and Toby promised him they would be very careful and never leave the house without Gabriel, or another responsible adult. Daisy cried a little and Toby was silent for an hour. The partings were becoming more and more unbearable as danger loomed ever closer.

Treefall set in, turning the dying leaves russet and gold. The pale sun shone through them as they became transparent, then finally dropped from their branches. Raven had already purchased waxed coats to keep out the rain and wind, as well as wool gloves, hats and scarves for all three. The Order of Lumen had, as usual, thought of everything, making sure that her guests were as comfortable as possible.

So far, Dark Star had not tried to invade the college, but one day, a friendly shepherd brought news of hikers with binoculars out on the moor - strangers who appeared to be observing Falconhurst from a distance. Raven asked him to keep a watchful eye out and bring news immediately if there were any new developments.

"We can't be too careful. Falconhurst is a long way off the beaten track, but Maxwell Delano was once a student here, before he turned bad, so he does know our location. Let's hope it's too far back in his memory to be of any consequence."

The observatory, which had become one of Toby's favourite places, had one complete wall made of glass, affording a spectacular view of both sea and sky. There were numerous shelves full of maps, charts and Eli's collection of reference books. The two large tables where he had been working earlier on were piled with papers and drawing instruments. Four very worn, leather studded armchairs had been arranged to allow a terrific view of the ocean.

Eli invited Toby and Daisy to take turns looking through the telescope, and one evening in the observatory, he taught them about a particular constellation of stars.

"Can you see, the shape of five major stars crossed in four directions with one exceptionally bright star at the centre and four at equal distances around it. The central star is a little bigger than the other four." Eli then drew the shape joining up the stars to form the cross, like one of those join the dots puzzles. Finally, he enclosed the pattern in a circle. "This constellation is called Harmony Wheel," he explained. "It's the home of our Lumerin and this shape forms the emblem of the Order of Lumen."

They also learned that, just as Harmony Wheel had five major stars, so Lumenor had five main continents.

"We're in Heartland," he told them, "like the central star. Across the sea to the north is Alba, to the east is Eos, the south Somerlin and to the west is Westernesse. Most of the Order of Lumen live in Heartland, to be at the centre, but there are still pockets of us scattered across the four outlands and islands, wherever there's a need for our skills or a place of special interest to us."

"Do you mean that Lumenor is like a reflection of the Harmony Wheel constellation?" asked Toby, looking at the diagram.

"Correct!" Eli smiled with approval.

"We're all proud of our Toby, he's the family boffin."

"Thanks Daise, that makes me happy because you don't want to change me anymore."

"Don't mention it pal."

When Gabriel and Raven joined them in the observatory, Eli retrieved the leather pouch he had hidden behind the tallest of the astrology volumes. He tipped the contents into Gabriel's open hand. "The Stone of Wisdom," he announced. The violet hue, rich as a royal robe, contained hidden depths that went on forever.

"It looks like it ought to be up there in the sky, with the stars," said Daisy, who couldn't take her eyes off the glowing purple gem.

"Maybe some of the light from the stars is already inside it," Raven replied, "and that's what you can see."

When they had all finished admiring it, Gabriel returned the jewel to its pouch before stowing it safely in the bag on his belt. He noticed a familiar, tiny knot of fear gnawing at him in a deep place. It never went away permanently, even though he was skilled at keeping his mind positive.

"Only one more to go," he murmured under his breath as the others began to leave the room. "Only one more to go, and then it's really going to happen. I do so hope I won't be found scared and wanting when the time comes to face Maxwell Delano."

23 EXPLOSION

Towards the end of their time at Falconhurst the changing weather turned the watery blue sky to leaden grey. The ocean pounded the eastern cliffs without mercy and the wind carried the salty, damp drizzle on to the moors and beyond. Because it was now dark at five-thirty, the Lantern Ceremonies were timed much earlier and always around the indoor lantern in the Greening Room for the safety of the guests. No one wanted to take any risks at this point in the quest.

Toby, Daisy and Gabriel spent most of their time inside, only venturing out for a few minutes' fresh air in the quadrangle. Board games and reading replaced football and croquet. Gabriel began to teach the cousins the basics of ancient Lumen, whilst Raven told them stories from the Legends of Lumenor. They often joined Eli in the evenings to observe the night sky. It all helped to pass the time.

"I have to say, Toby, that I never enjoyed school so much in my life," remarked Daisy.

"Me neither, I especially love the Observatory, I never thought about spending time looking at stars before, I mean you can see the night sky on the Internet or the telly but this is a real experience."

"I'm glad you've been happy here," said Raven, "everyone learns when they're interested. And now, would you like to sing the Heartsong for me again?" And so, they sang it every day, never forgetting the words and adding a little more feeling as the chant to the brightest of the Lumerin became a part of them.

On the forty-eighth day of Treefall, the decorators came in a van, unloading tarpaulins, paint and ladders. Raven had decided that it was a perfect opportunity to have the empty study rooms painted in time for the return of her adult students.

"I am certain that you should leave in the next few days," she advised Gabriel. "Each day, there are new walkers on the moor and they're coming ever closer to the house, according to my shepherd friend. The two decorators bring their van here every day at nine in the morning and leave at four. In three days you'll be going with them."

Thinking it sounded like a good plan, Gabriel agreed, though he wasn't exactly sure how that would get them to their next destination in the north.

After Toby and Daisy had been given the news of an imminent departure, Raven outlined the Lumerin's plan.

"The decorator will transport you ten miles to the canal at Linden Bridge, where a narrow boat had been organized. It belongs to Taylor Beech, He uses it when he wants to chill out and be on his own. Here are the keys."

"Yes, I've met Taylor," Gabriel remembered, "at the Allegria Hotel a couple of years ago. Easy going sort of bloke. I can just picture him on a narrow boat."

"Your route lies to the north along the canal, to a mooring close to the Fox and Grapes Hotel in the market town of Dellaby. Here, you will be met by car, and taken on to the next destination where you will pick up the seventh and final stone."

"Where's that?" asked Toby."

"Can't tell you," was Raven's answer. "I'm not too sure, and anyway you can only know just before you begin that journey. Lumerin precautions."

Leaving Falconhurst proved to be one of their most difficult departures, because the weather was much colder with the approach of Earthstill. It would already be dark when they arrived at the canal. Fully togged up in their new coats and woolies, Gabriel, Toby and Daisy slipped into the rear space of the decorator's van, which had been backed up to an open door around the side of the building.

"It's going to take about half an hour," the driver said. "I'm sorry if it's a bit uncomfortable."

"No problem at all." There wasn't much room for Gabriel's long legs, but he appreciated the help and preferred not to complain.

The narrow boat sat low in the water at its mooring in Linden Bridge. By the time they arrived, it was already too dark to admire the bright yellow and blue flowers painted on to the crimson background, or the name Clementine scrolled in emerald.

"I want to get off this towpath!" Unlocking the door Gabriel ushered them aboard. "Quick as you can there too many shadowy bushes where enemies can conceal themselves and launch a surprise attack. Can you hear that owl Toby?"

"It's okay," Toby sighed with relief. "The owl is sure that there's nobody here we need to worry about and that we are not in any immediate danger, but he's also keen to remind us that we shouldn't get careless at any time on this trip."

Daisy clambered through the doorway into the narrow interior, with the others following closely. "Who's going to drive it, Gabriel?" she asked.

"I am, of course," he said, smiling, "as soon as the sun's up. I had a holiday on one of these once. It's a lot of fun."

"I don't want any fun right now," Daisy whined. "I just want to get to the next stone."

"Pay attention to the journey, Daisy." Gabriel was stern with her. "That's all there is at the moment, so make the best of it. Thinking about the next stone will only make you nervous, believe me, I know - I've tried it."

Daisy let out a long suffering groan, and went off alone to explore the boat.

Someone had provided a very good stock of provisions including an enormous box of chocolate biscuits. There was even a portable gas ring and a kettle in a kitchen area and each of them had a small bedroom leading off a communal seating space. As the facilities were so much better than Daisy had expected, her mood soon changed.

For the next five days, a pale sun showed its cheery face to warm their journey as the narrow boat sailed slowly down the canal with a contented Gabriel at the tiller. Toby and Daisy were eager to learn how to steer and help with the lock gates. A new routine developed, slowing life down to the pace of the boat. Toby said that he had never paid so much attention his surroundings, because like most boys of his age, he always had so much to do. Now, he saw every tree, every bird and all the sharp seasonal colours nature had to offer, from the deck of this slow boat to Dellaby.

At sunset, they moored, ate and slept, rising with the late Treefall sun and sailing until it set again. It was a pleasant and undemanding time, though Gabriel secretly kept his eyes peeled for signs of Dark Star spies. After five whole days and nights, there had been no evidence of anything unusual or dangerous. On the sixth night, only one day away from their destination they stopped in place named Wishburn and retired to their rooms. As always after a day in the fresh air, it wasn't long before sleep overtook them.

Toby dreamed of woodland - warm, green and filled with sweet birdsong. He was sitting comfortably under a leafy oak chatting to squirrels when he saw the unicorn.

"Rio!" It was a happy reunion, even in a dream.

Now the unicorn's face seemed to be right in front of him, as golden sparks bounced off his forehead.

"Wake up, Toby! Wake up! You have to get out of here now!" It wasn't a suggestion. It was a command.

Toby opened his eyes, leaping from his bunk like a sprinter from the starting blocks. He ran first to Gabriel's room and then to Daisy's, yelling like crazy.

"Get up! Get up! Rio says we have to get off the Clementine
. We have to dress and grab our stuff now!"

Neither of the other two questioned the logic of the sudden
awakening, because Toby's unicorn dreams had been spot on
before. Soon, wrapped up warmly and carrying rucksacks, they
were clambering hastily off the Clementine.

Running like the clappers, they found a welcome clump of
bushes to conceal them, just off the towpath and about a
hundred yards away from the prow of the boat. Huddled close
together, they waited, silent and still, trying to slow their
breathing and wondering what was coming next. They didn't
have long to wait and in fact, a delay of even five minutes
leaving that boat would have spelled total disaster.

From their hiding place, Gabriel, Toby and Daisy had a view
of the towpath and the Clementine. The distant sound of voices
drifted towards them, as two beams of light danced along the
canal, outlining the dark shape of the narrow boat.

"I do believe that's Irina Slack and Hugo Shade with three
other men," groaned Gabriel, straining to see. He concentrated
a little harder. "Yes," he sounded more confident, "looks like
Planks, Scally, and Mackintosh."

"How could those losers possibly have found us?" whispered
Daisy disturbed at the turn of events.

"Don't know." Gabriel didn't take his eyes off the scene on
the towpath.

Sid Planks began to unzip the large canvas bag he had just
placed on the ground.

"Let's have a butchers through your binoculars, Gabriel?"
Daisy was impatient to get a better look.

"Unfortunately, they're right at the bottom of my rucksack,
which I can't risk unpacking right now," he replied sadly.

Hugo Shade barked some orders, though he was too far away
for Gabriel to hear what they were. Next, Sid, Jack and Barry
climbed on to the barge and began placing whatever they had in
their hands on various parts of the deck. After the job was
done, Jack Scally remained on the Clementine as the other four

walked quickly away and were soon out of sight.

"They've obviously parked their evil Jag in a lane somewhere down the canal," reasoned Daisy. "What do you suppose that creep Scally's doing?"

"Not sure," Gabriel replied, "but I do know I have a very bad feeling about it."

In an instant, Jack Scally jumped off the boat and ran down the towpath as fast as a hunting cheetah.

Seconds later, a terrifying boom and an orange fireball rent the night apart as the unfortunate Clementine exploded into a million fragments of matchwood and metal. It was so loud that it almost shattered their eardrums. All three fell backwards, covering their heads with their arms to protect themselves from flying debris. There was a terrible acrid smell as a thick pall of smoke blocked out the canal.

Their survival instincts kicked in, forcing a quick recovery.

"They really did mean to kill us then ..." Toby's voice faltered. "I didn't seriously think they'd do that. It's unreal."

"Well, now you know just how real it is. They certainly are prepared to commit murder to stop us from interfering with their grand plans. We're dealing with evil on a scale beyond your experience and you've yet to meet Maxwell Delano."

Daisy, also in shock, was in danger of bursting into tears, when another beam of light appeared, moving towards them from the other direction. Scrambling to their feet, they prepared to fight this new threat.

"I'm a friend," said the stranger, shining the torch beam on his own wizened face so that Gabriel could get a good look.

"Ellery Bright!" Gabriel relaxed. "How did you know?"

"Let's just say - I've had instructions," explained the newcomer. "My house is just a mile away. I'm pretty certain that Dark Star has already pushed off, keen to get away from the scene of their appalling crime. The explosion was so spectacular I expect someone's already called the police."

"Which is why we have to vamoose," Gabriel insisted. "We can't afford the time to get caught up in police enquiries. It would only complicate matters. Lead the way, Ellery!"

Until this night, Toby had never thought just how precious his life was. Thank goodness Rio had walked into his dream.

"We've had a very lucky escape," whimpered Daisy.

"There's no luck involved," replied Gabriel. "It all depends on the strength of your connection."

The fugitives made their escape from the canal just as a small crowd began arriving to find out what was going on. The police, who had missed their hasty exit by only three minutes, set about questioning the people gathering on the towpath, but apart from the explosion itself, nobody had seen anything or had a clue whether anyone had been on board the boat when it went up. After a walk along a lane, across a dark field and two tree-lined streets, Ellery led them through his garden gate to a bungalow surrounded by conifers, where Selena Bright ushered them in like a caring mother hen.

"Two in the morning." Gabriel glanced wearily at the carriage clock on the mantelpiece above the beige tiled fireplace. He had to admit to himself that he was feeling shaken but he needed to keep it together for Toby and Daisy's sake.

"Dark Star certainly keep inconvenient times," complained Selena. "I've telephoned your next destination and a car's coming here for you later this morning."

Daisy couldn't help eyeing the two old people closely as she drank her hot, sweet tea, fortified with a dose of Shock Buster. In spite of their lined faces and thinning white hair, the couple were blessed with an unusual air of strength and vitality. Not your usual sort of pensioners, she thought.

Ellery smiled as he picked up her feeling. "I am one hundred and two years old," he announced proudly, "and Selena is one hundred and one. Because of our connection to the Lumerin, members of our Order can live to around one hundred and twenty. At only twenty-eight, Gabriel, here, is just a boy."

Daisy's jaw dropped as she stared first at Gabriel and then at Ellery – twenty-eight did seem pretty damn old to her, but one hundred and twenty was absolutely historical. Having said that, she and Toby had just escaped being blown to bits at only eleven. She could certainly see why they had to stop Delano.

"I don't want to be morbid," said Toby, downcast, "but I can't help wondering what would've happened if we'd been blown up on that barge."

"Well, now," said Ellery, deep in thought, "a former lantern maker, I've learned a lot in my time, and my present understanding tells me that Gabriel would have simply become pure Lumerin. You, of course, might also have become the same, except that if you have a destiny in the place you came from, then you would likely have woken up back there, without the slightest notion that any of this had happened. So you see, Toby, it's not morbid at all."

Toby was suitably cheered by the simple, unexpected explanation.

"However," Ellery continued, "that would most certainly have meant the failure of your quest to get back the Heart of Stars, and then the end of Lumenor as we know it, and that is a very big thing." Hanging his head, he added, "I couldn't bear to see all my beautiful lanterns destroyed by black light."

"Bedtime for the two youngest," said Selena, preparing to usher them away along the corridor towards the two spare rooms.

After arranging his pillow and blankets on the sitting room couch, Gabriel took a torch to check the garden before turning in, but the darkened world was silent except for the natural sounds of its nocturnal creatures. *It might prove to be safe for the time being, if Dark Star thinks we're dead. This is an unexpected, but very welcome bonus after such a close shave*, he thought, *perhaps Hugo Shade and Irina Slack are celebrating somewhere.*

It was the first time that Gabriel had been able to relax his guard since their departure from the Allegria Hotel and even though the couch wasn't quite long enough and his feet were sticking over the end, he was soon asleep.

24 THE FESTIVAL OF EARTHSTILL

The plain blue van arrived to fetch them at exactly eleven o'clock .

"Be sure to give our kind regards to Brigit," said Ellery to Gabriel, who was just draining the last mouthful of tea from his mug.

"Brigit?' queried Toby, "who's Brigit?".

"My mother, of course," said Gabriel with a wide smile. "And here's my big brother."

Leo Greenway unfolded himself from the driver's seat of the van and bounded through the open door, catching Gabriel in a happy bear hug. Toby and Daisy, never thinking that they would ever meet Gabriel's family, were very excited to be introduced and wanted to know everything about him.

Leo, seven years older than Gabriel, and the father of two young children, was slightly shorter and fairer than his brother, but with the same merry, brown eyes. He had always lived and worked at Sylvanhay, the Greenway's farming estate in the village of Owlthorpe, whilst Gabriel, with a very different destiny, had left for Robinswood to pursue his own calling. There was also a younger sister Elen, who was away in Eos studying wildlife, but expected home in time for the Earthstill Festival.

Travelling northwest through Lumenor's Heartland, the

journey took nearly three hours. Fertile acres of dry-walled farmland stretched beyond the yard of a large farmhouse which gave the appearance of a small manor. The Dairy herds grazed in abundant pastures, whilst fat sheep, all cozy in their thick white fleeces, dotted the more distant hillsides.

"That's my cottage over there!" Leo pointed out a smaller stone house to Toby and Daisy. "My wife, Hazel, can't wait to meet you and neither can our mother."

"What about our father? " Gabriel asked.

"Don't you remember?" Leo sounded surprised. "He was called to Ynys yr Delyn on the thirtieth day of Treefall because he's destined to lead the Order for a year. He won't be able to visit us until the lambing time."

Gabriel had completely forgotten, following the stressful events in Mornington. "It had gone right out of my mind," he sighed. "We've been caught up in stuff like you can't imagine Leo, and I haven't been able to think about anything else. Life has been far from normal for ages."

"I'm sorry," replied Leo gently, "and you're right. I can't possibly imagine what it's been like, but I've thought about you a great deal if that's any consolation."

Gabriel looked contented. It was a very good feeling to be close to his brother again.

Brigit Greenway's welcome could not have been warmer, as Leo showed Toby and Daisy into the bright rear sitting room, with its tall sash windows and high ceilings. The squashy, gold brocade sofas and matching drapes created a cheerful, sunny atmosphere. Oriental rugs with symmetrical patterns adorned the varnished oak floorboards, dampening the sound of their footsteps.

Brigit, her chestnut hair pulled back into a French pleat and wearing a sweater dress of rich emerald green, fitted perfectly into her beautiful environment. With tears in her eyes, she threw her arms around Gabriel, remarking how tired he looked. She then fussed over Daisy and Toby, pulling them towards one of the sofas to sit next to her.

"I see that you've lots of sheep and cattle here," remarked Toby, who never missed an opportunity to talk about animals.

"We certainly have," replied Brigit. "There are also cows, horses, goats, chickens, ducks and geese for you to meet during your stay." Being a senior member of the Order of Lumen, she was well aware of Toby's special talent. "All of these animals are wonderful gifts, which we never take for granted. For example, take the humble sheep - it gives us wool and hide for clothing and furnishings, milk and meat - and the cow is similarly generous yet it doesn't occur to most people to give thanks for the blessing of these special creatures. I mean seriously, how often do you remember a hen when you eat an egg? It's the ordinary magic, which comes into our lives every day reminding us of our connection to the land, the sky and all life. We just have to take a little time to notice it."

"I resolve right now never to take things for granted." Toby made a vow. "In fact, I fully intend to give some of Sylvanhay's animals a personal thank you if I am allowed to go outside." He thought about the sun and the rain turning the seeds into flowers and then Gabriel's friend Sage in her garden. "I want to make my connection stronger, to notice all this ordinary magic and make myself part of it."

"Good, we shall be staying until the morning of the tenth day of Earthstill which gives us an entire month before we begin the most difficult and threatening part of our journey," Gabriel became serious," then, we face the final part of our mission... steal back the Heart of Stars and save Lumenor for generations to come."

The smiles left Daisy's face as soon as she began to think about the reason for their journey north and once again that awful memory of the exploding boat returned to upset her.

"I feel like I'm living in a computer game where you have to zap the bad guy before he zaps you," complained Toby.

"What's a computer game?" Gabriel asked, taking a new remedy labelled Light Wave from the box in his rucksack.

"Don't worry about it, they haven't been invented here yet."

"If you say so," Gabriel answered. "Now, take some of these drops. One dose should cheer you up and make you altogether more upbeat. It contains some of that water from Oriel Solana's sunny well."

Once the good mood had been restored, Brigit removed a small silver box from the antique cabinet, in which she kept a few of her special things. "I only brought it into the house this morning," she announced. "It has been well hidden until today." Removing the customary leather pouch, she gave it to Gabriel, who held its contents up to the light so that the others could get a good look.

"Wow!" Leo expressed genuine surprise. "I've never actually seen this gem before, even though it's been here for some time."

"Seems like I'm the only Greenway who didn't know it was here, Leo."

"Not so, bro, Hazel and the kids don't know, Elen doesn't know and surprisingly neither does Dad."

"Don't tell me…"

"LUMERIN PRECAUTIONS!" they all chorused.

"The Stone of Plenty," announced Brigit once the laughter had subsided. "It's sometimes called the Harvest or Celebration Stone."

The vibrant green of the jewel spread out filling the entire room as the last of the afternoon light passed through it from the window. Contained within its emerald glow, the shapes of nature spirits appeared translucent and winged as they emerged and flew around the room, alighting on shoulders and heads before disappearing with a 'pop' like bubbles.

In his mind's eye, Toby saw an image of a Christmas tree hung with baubles and candy, whilst Daisy's vision was a long table set with a feast. Gabriel heard music and laughter followed by a sudden picture of a splendid sunrise, which he hoped was a good omen for a bright Threshold. Gradually, as the images faded, he returned the stone to its pouch, before placing it with the others in the bag on his belt.

"Well, now," Brigit's mood was cheerful. "We'll celebrate our Earthstill Festival together, as we always do. I won't allow the likes of Maxwell Delano to take away our fun. We can begin the decorations tomorrow, and I think it best if we all stay out of the village, just in case Dark Star's snooping around. The people who work for us here are all Order of Lumen, either living on the estate or in Owlthorpe, so we'll have a good many watching eyes of our own."

"Is that why the village is called Owlthorpe?" Daisy smiled sweetly.

Toby gave his cousin a long-suffering look, but the news about the decorations had made her too happy to notice.

The following morning, a tall fir tree planted in a wide pot arrived, accompanied by a heap of assorted greenery consisting of holly with red berries, mistletoe, and conifer garlands. There were also satin ribbons, silver and gold paint for the pinecones and a large, mysterious wooden box with a robin painted on it. This was Daisy's idea of total perfection; Toby also wasted no time in getting into the festive spirit.

"Open the box," said Gabriel. "All my memories of past Earthstill Festivals are inside it."

And so the treasure chest revealed its contents to two excited young people. Some of the decorations, Gabriel explained, had been in the Greenway family for generations, appearing like old friends as Daisy pulled them out one by one to lay them carefully on the table by the tree. There were wassail cups, bells and globes of fine glass, some of them frosted with snow. There were doves, owls, reindeer, stags, squirrels, robins and only one white wooden unicorn, which Gabriel hung near the top of the tree, just below the glittering star, which sat at the very top.

Although the festival wasn't called Christmas, Christmas was exactly the experience that Toby and Daisy were having. But then, there were always those things in Lumenor, which just seemed oddly familiar. It felt so good to be part of a family again.

All kinds of goodies began to appear on the stone shelves of the pantry just off the kitchen. Toby's mouth watered each time he went to check out what new things had been baked. So far, he had been allowed to taste mince pies, jam tarts, almond tarts and fruit-cake. The latest arrivals were pink sugar mice and marzipan fruits, which, of course, had to be sampled in their turn.

"Is the whole village coming?" asked Daisy. "There's enough in the pantry to feed an army."

"Definitely! Always do!" said a plump little woman called Lavinia who had come to help with the baking. "It's tradition for the Order of Lumen to meet here on Earthstill Festival Eve to celebrate together, and of course after the food, there will be dancing to fiddle and flute, piano, guitar and drum."

It was the most fun two young people could possibly experience, knowing that they were living the last days of calm before the inevitable storm.

On Festival Eve, Sylvanhay hosted a very special Lantern Ceremony. Order of Lumen friends arrived in their hooded, wool robes of cobalt blue with the emblem of Harmony Wheel embroidered on the front in white, its stars depicted in gold silken thread. Everyone present carried a copper lantern housing a white candle. As each lamp was ignited and held aloft, the lights resembled a swarm of dancing fireflies.

"It's completely awesome!" Toby was spellbound.

"I don't think I've ever seen anything so totally beautiful." Daisy was stunned by the grace of the ancient ritual as the singing began.

It seemed as though the sky blazed and the stars fell to Earth as the Order of Lumen encircled the Great Lantern, singing in perfect harmony. The Lumerin floated around the merry makers like butterflies, infusing the crystal with their bright presence.

"I could swear that there are colours I've never seen before," said Daisy. "Unfortunately, because I have never seen them before and they don't have names, I can't describe them to anyone"

Once the lantern was ignited and the ceremony came to an end, the line of merrymakers, singing all the while, filed into the house led by Brigit in her position as festival host. At last, all the hard work of the past two weeks was laid out on tables like the feast that Daisy had seen in the Stone of Plenty. According to tradition, the Greenways and all their guests linked hands to give thanks for the gifts of good food and good company before sitting down for their celebration meal. It was a memorable evening of laughter, dancing, kindness and contentment when Toby and Daisy experienced an official welcome into the greater family of the Order of Lumen.

The following day after breakfast, Leo, Hazel and their two little ones Bonnie and Arthur joined the rest of the family in the sitting room. Three days earlier, the return of Gabriel's sister, Elen, had brought great joy and Daisy had felt an immediate bond with her because with the exception of her dark brown hair, Elen was so much like her mother in both manner and looks. Daisy bagged the seat next to her on one of the sofas.

Brigit handed out presents from under the tree, something that Toby and Daisy had not expected for themselves. Their parcels revealed gifts from the Sylvanhay flocks: sheepskin waistcoats, thick socks, fleece lined boots, and natural wool sweaters, which Hazel had made herself. Gabriel who had received the same seemed a little overwhelmed. "Can't tell you how pleased I am to have this little bit of home to keep me warm when the time comes to face the frozen breath of Dark Star."

"I wish we could have gone out to get things for all of you," said Daisy wistfully.

"We don't need things," Elen reassured her. "You're already giving of yourselves to help us to save our world, and that's more than enough." There was an immediate chorus of agreement.

"Do you know," said Toby, "whatever happens, I would still be willing to repeat the whole experience, if only for the time spent at Sylvanhay, and the magic of just one Earthstill

Festival."

They passed the rest of the day sitting around the fire telling stories. Elen gave vivid descriptions of her travels in Eos, and later in the evening, Leo played the piano to complete the entertainment.

"We've only eight more days before Delano," Daisy reminded her cousin.

"Mmm. D–Day." Toby's laugh sounded hollow. Right now, he was unwilling to spoil his fun by letting the enemy into his mind. "Let's just have a good time, Daise, and think about that when it happens," he said, attempting to change the subject.

25 ANGWISH CASTLE

The happiness following the festival was indeed short lived, as the dreaded eve of departure arrived all too soon and Brigit had received unwelcome news.

"The Order of Lumen Elders, are now certain that Maxwell Delano has found the remaining verses of the terrible chant to corrupt the Heart of Stars. That obscure prophecy we discovered will soon be put to the test. There can be no going back, but remember, it is all still to play for. Gabriel, we're counting on you!"

Frosty days dawned bright and crisp with some strong sunshine around late morning, but then, in the afternoon, the temperature plunged, forcing Daisy and Toby indoors after lunch but still no snow appeared.

"I can feel it in the air," Leo insisted, "and unfortunately, I predict a heavy fall by Threshold. What do the Lumerin say Gabriel and what are your plans?"

"I understand that Delano has purchased a semi ruined castle in an isolated spot due north of Sylvanhay. Its position is about two miles outside the nearest village. The very name, Angwish Castle, sounds sinister, depressing and painful. The Eve of Threshold will be no holiday Leo, but then I have always known that."

After Toby and Daisy had retired to their beds, Gabriel was

glad of the opportunity to spend a little time alone with Brigit. The company of his mother was always a pleasure. Relaxing on the sofa in front of the crackling fire, they enjoyed a glass of elderberry wine together with the last of the festival cake.

"I'm keeping my mind in the present, just as you've always taught me," Gabriel told her, "but I'm sorry to say… I can feel a small knot of fear deep inside. Do you have any suggestions?"

"Please don't try to fix that, but equally don't allow it to grow and overwhelm you. It's there to alert you to pay attention to this extraordinary situation you're facing. Treat it as a friend."

Gabriel sighed and was silent for a while, reflecting on her words as he stared into the dancing flames of the living room fire. "Apart from being my mother, you are a very wise woman and a respected Elder. Your advice has always been sound, so I will do as you say."

"You know," Brigit continued, "each day, I've dedicated a small portion of time to just thinking about you, ever since you left home. On Threshold Eve, I shall do the same. The Order of Lumen everywhere has instructions to join together and focus on your task. Everyone we know will be here at midnight to light their lanterns, just as they did for the festival. We'll sing to hold you in as much light as possible, and the same thing will be happening all over Lumenor wherever our kind exists. If you remember this, it will be like drawing a protective cloak around you to keep out Dark Star's icy blast."

"Your words are comforting," replied Gabriel, "of course everyone will try to support and assist us. Why didn't I think of that?"

"I confess that when you were chosen to look after the Harp Children, I wished that it could have been anyone's son but my own. In time, I accepted it as your destiny, along with the understanding that being your mother has been a major part of mine. It's no longer a question of why, but how to make it work."

"I've decided to leave the seven harp stones at Sylvanhay. If anything should go wrong, then they, at least, will not be lost."

"Wise choice," agreed Brigit, "though if I remember rightly, the prophecy only talks about two young ones coming in a time of great need. I don't recall it saying that they wouldn't succeed. However, I do sense that Toby is going to find Delano's appalling magic more distressing than either you or Daisy so look after him carefully. In the meantime, I'll keep the stones safe until you return to collect them."

"Thanks, Mum." Gabriel planted an affectionate kiss on her cheek. "I'd better get some sleep now. There's a difficult day ahead."

Brigit felt a deep sense of pride welling up inside her as she watched him leave the room.

The morning of departure arrived in the wake of a very cold and cutting north wind. The sheep on the hillside huddled together, waiting for the snowfall. One of the farm jeeps had already been checked and packed ready for departure.

"What if the snow's heavy and we get stuck?" Toby became obsessive. "We have to be there at the right time. What if we're late?"

"In that unlikely event, someone will come for you," Brigit assured him. "The people expecting you have been given an estimated time of arrival."

Toby stopped worrying and picked up his rucksack, which, with only one change of clothes as well as his torch, compass and the pair of binoculars Elen had given him, was now considerably lighter. Gabriel had also packed his special potions and a small first aid kit, just in case.

"We'll be back here in two days," he announced cheerfully. "Count on it!"

Keeping their goodbyes short to avoid becoming too emotional, they made a swift departure. Even Toby and Daisy had understood that clear thinking and sound instincts were now of the utmost importance to their mission.

"Pass me the map Gabriel, I'd like to navigate because it will keep my mind occupied and then I'll forget to worry, it's only sixty miles," Toby calculated, "so we should be there in no time."

"That's always provided Dark Star haven't realized that we weren't wiped out when they blew up the Clementine, right." Daisy was worried, haunted again by her memory of the narrow boat explosion.

"Don't go there," Gabriel was firm with her. "I've brought a bottle of that special Light Wave potion, which contains water from Oriel's well, but I'd rather not use it all up before we even arrive. Remember your training."

Daisy sighed deeply. She had forgotten again. It seemed such a long time since Ynys Arian.

Around midday, they arrived at a small guesthouse in the market town of Bridgeway where the owner, a mature lady called Angelica Swan had hot soup waiting for them. Angelica explained that she was a more recent member of the Order of Lumen.

"The ideas about the stars came on ever so gradually, well, over many seasons really, and just when I was wondering whom I could talk to, I met Tristan Wilde. It must be all of three years ago just after Threshold in the year 2202 - yes, he moved here almost three years ago to open an antiquarian bookshop, and since then, I've never looked back. You'll meet him tonight because he's going to show you the way to that terrible place up by the crags. It's supposed to be haunted, by the way."

Daisy and Toby looked at each other and smiled.

"It's a laugh," said Daisy, "I'm not worried about ghosts, because they'll probably be as scared of Dark Star as we are."

At around five, there was a loud rap on the front door. Tristan Wilde, a tall, jolly bear of a man, with bushy red hair and a matching beard, lumbered into the lounge. Handing his overcoat and tweed cap to Angelica, he removed his bicycle clips before claiming the spare armchair close to the fire.

"Tomorrow, at sunset, as instructed, we're going to Angwish Castle. It isn't a real castle, you know, it's a folly, less than two hundred years old, though only part of it is habitable nowadays.

It's no accident that I'm here. I arrived in Bridgeway, not long after Delano bought it."

"It's lucky, then, that Angelica needed you," said Toby.

"I haven't just come to help Angelica, although sometimes things do tend to work out in an extraordinary way. Apart from selling antique books, you could say that I'm a spy. Like Gabriel, I was born into an old Order of Lumen family, so I've never known any other life. I go where it's necessary for me to be at any given time. I've been watching the comings and goings at Angwish for ages now and have found out a great deal. Delano's lot have been here for about for four weeks, though nobody has set eyes on the man himself."

During an extensive and well-planned snooping campaign, Tristan had discovered that the old gamekeeper's cottage at Angwish Castle was deserted. On his one and only visit, Delano had looked round, noted its sorry dilapidated state and decided to ignore its existence. However, the old maps, which Tristan had tracked down through his many contacts, showed something Max didn't know about, a secret passage leading from the lodge's basement to the old wine cellar, located below the Butler's Pantry in the castle's former kitchens.

"I am told," he explained, "the first Lord Angwish, who was as nasty as they come - a smuggler and gambler, by all accounts - had the lodge and the passage built so that he could get in and out without being seen."

"Too cool!" Toby's interest rose at the mention of another secret passage. "This one sounds so much more exciting than the connecting basement rooms in Mornington, but a million times more risky."

"I doubt if it's going to be any fun, Toby," Daisy glowered, "or have you forgotten what's at the other end of the tunnel?"

"Don't argue, that's an order. "Don't open any doors in your heads where Dark Star can walk in and create havoc. How many times do I have to say it?" Gabriel was beginning to sound just a little stressed.

"Here we go again!" Scowling at the reprimand, Daisy gave

in. She knew she had to keep making an effort.

After Tristan left, the house seemed very quiet, so Angelica suggested watching TV to pass the time and, luckily, one of the only two channels available in Lumenor was showing a half hour comedy followed by a suitable quiz programme. Before today, there hadn't been much time for watching television. Life had been so full on that the out of date, black and white pictures on strange, small screens had ceased to be an issue as long ago as Oaklands. Even the daily happenings in Daisy's favourite soap had been forgotten. They finished the day playing dominoes with Gabriel, and turned in early to try to get as much sleep as possible.

On Threshold Eve, the travellers awoke to a white, shrouded world. The fresh snow, almost blinding in the morning sunlight, had covered pathways and fields in a soft, silent carpet. On any other day, Toby and Daisy would have been excited by such a heavy snowfall, but on this occasion, it seemed like one more obstacle on top of an already overwhelming burden.

This dreaded day, once an unreal, future event, had finally arrived in the present, leaving no time for snowball fights, building snowmen or anything else entertaining for that matter. After a hot lunch of shepherd's pie, they talked through their plans until Tristan arrived.

Wrapped up warm, in their new sheepskin things and waxed coats, Toby and Daisy put their torches in their pockets and, for the first time, left the rucksacks behind. Only Gabriel carried luggage containing a little food and his special potions. They were in for a long, anxious night, without knowing exactly what awaited them at Angwish Castle.

"Take this," he said, administering a dose of Light Wave and another one of something called Heat Wave. "These potions should keep you positive and warm inside for a long time, though I have to warn you that Delano's atmosphere will be difficult, even with the potions. You'll still need to watch your thoughts and keep your coats on."

The silent, white fields had begun to freeze after the second snowfall. Tonight, there was no friendly moon to light their path, and the stars, which seemed so far away, felt as cold as the frosty land. Daisy searched the heavens for a comforting glimpse of Harmony Wheel, but failed to find it.

They followed Tristan on and on as he crunched his way across the snow, confident and surefooted with Gabriel bringing up the rear, to keep a look out behind. Nobody spoke until Tristan stopped to draw the group together under the ghostly branches of a snow- laden tree.

"See that?" he said, pointing to a dark mass, which was just visible against the untouched snow. A couple of lights gleamed from the black shape in the distance.

"That's Angwish Castle, it's about a quarter of a mile away," he whispered. "We now have to skirt around the field and then walk down the lane to the gamekeeper's lodge."

"We'll take it slowly," added Gabriel, who was becoming aware that he didn't have a list of instructions from the Lumerin as to what exactly had to happen when they reached the final destination.

"It's great that you have that skeleton key from Michael Dory," said Tristan, "because it means that I don't have to break the door."

"I have it here, safe in my waistcoat pocket." Gabriel patted his chest to make sure.

The disused lodge looked forlorn and frozen, as the last of the day finally slipped through the far end of twilight, into the shadows of the final night of the year. Although the door was difficult to open and Tristan had to light a match to unfreeze the lock, they were soon safe within the dim, neglected interior.

"Oh, gross!" Daisy brushed aside the cobwebs dangling in her face and hair. Tristan closed the door behind them and checked that the shutters were in place on the windows. When he was sure that nobody could possibly be watching, they all switched on their torches. There was a strong smell of damp to go with the cobwebs and crumbling furniture; it was as if the place had just been locked up one day, and then left to decay.

"Do you suppose this is the haunted bit?" Toby asked Tristan.

"No. People say that the ghost of a young man haunts the crags at the back of the main house - a young man killed by his brother, the first Lord of Angwish. I shouldn't worry about it if I were you, because you'll have enough to do tonight without spook hunting. Now, let me see"… he said, leading them towards the back of the lodge, … "according to the maps, the scullery is this way, and the door to the cellar is in the scullery."

The battered, brown door swung open easily, revealing stone steps leading down into invisible depths. One by one, they descended without a sound, until they reached the cold flagstones of the unknown room below.

"Here it is." Tristan directed his torch beam to the wall directly opposite the steps, "there are four panels of empty wooden shelving stretching in a row, from the floor to just below the ceiling …yes, that's exactly right… not a problem, the information's correct so far … and I believe it's the second panel to the left." Tristan walked off to examine that section of the shelving more closely. The others followed, tense with expectation, as they listened to him counting the shelves, beginning at the bottom and stopping at number five.

"Right! Let's hope all those old maps are accurate, shall we?" He ran his fingers slowly along the underside of the sixth shelf. There was a sharp click, and the shelving appeared to move away from the wall, creating a widening gap as Tristan pulled open the secret door, so cleverly attached to the shelving. The black hole of the tunnel gaped in front of them like the entrance to hell.

"This is well scary." Daisy's voice was a whisper as she grabbed hold of Gabriel's hand for reassurance.

"Totally spine tingling," agreed Toby, his words echoing into the black space. "This secret passage doesn't seem quite so cool anymore."

"I can't go any further with you," announced Tristan with regret. "You see, I'm not appointed to this task and my presence could change the outcome. I have to return home now to follow my own instructions."

"Wait a minute," Gabriel pleaded. "I know the ceremony to corrupt the Heart of Stars will take place in the Great Hall, but I haven't the slightest idea where that might be in the castle."

"The maps say the Great Hall's on the first floor to the left of the grand staircase," Tristan explained, " but you'll be climbing up from the wine cellar into the Butler's Pantry, adjacent to the old kitchens. I know Delano isn't using them, because I have it on the good authority from a local plumber that he had a new modern kitchen installed upstairs in the other wing only last year. Now, when you get to the old kitchens, take the servants' staircase, the one they used to take the meals to the banquets. It leads directly into the Great Hall."

"Thanks, Tris" Gabriel was grateful for his friend's thorough research. The Order of Lumen's teamwork really was a complete marvel.

"Good luck, and may the Lumerin light your way," came the reply as Tristan's bulky shape disappeared up the steps to the scullery. "See you tomorrow!" He sounded confident as he opened the battered, brown door at the top of the stairs and vanished into his own destiny.

The three of them were alone now, standing precariously on the edge of either a bright Threshold or the total destruction of Lumenor.

"Well this is it! Toby, Daisy – Let's go and steal ourselves a Heart of Stars shall we?"

Leaving the door ajar, they plunged into the open mouth of the tunnel, flooding its inky blackness with torchlight.

26 THE EVE OF THRESHOLD

"It's really cold in here. I'm freezing to death!" The temperature had dropped several degrees in the last two minutes. Daisy shivered as she followed Gabriel. The brick lined passage, with its arched roof, reminded her of a very narrow railway tunnel.

"At least it's dry," Gabriel observed. "I'm afraid that extreme cold is a particular effect associated with Maxwell Delano, something directly from the Dark Star beings he calls out of their frozen hell. Let's stop for a minute and take some more of that warming up potion."

Removing the bottle of Heat Wave from the familiar box, he gave Toby and Daisy six more drops each, before taking his own dose. He then administered some extra Light Wave as an added precaution.

"Whilst these potions will certainly lessen the Delano effect, I fear it's unlikely that they will totally block it out. It depends to what extent Dark Star has increased his power, and I'm afraid that nobody but Maxwell Delano has that knowledge," said Gabriel sounding uncertain. "We can only hope for the best."

Toby could easily have become panicky, as he did not like the confined space of the tunnel, but the Light Wave had already taken effect and he was eager to get going as soon he began to warm up from the inside. Pressing on towards their goal, their spirits lifted by the potions, they didn't stop until

Gabriel's torch beam illuminated an unexpected dead end in the form of a carved wooden panel depicting an ornate grape vine.

"And just how do we get through that, now Tristan's gone?" groaned Daisy.

"Just pipe down a minute, Daisy," Gabriel answered with some impatience. "Tristan has told me exactly what to do, so I just need to concentrate." Directing light on to the panel, Gabriel looked for the central bunch of grapes on the right hand side. "Here it is," He held his breath and pressed it quickly, exhaling in relief when the mechanism opened easily with a soft clunk.

Pushing the door panel to reveal a narrow gap, Gabriel peered into the total silence and complete darkness of the castle's old wine cellar. Confident now, he chanced a little torchlight, "It's clear, follow me, keep quiet and stay close." The wine cellar, unused and forlorn, was littered with empty bottles and broken wooden barrels. There was a smell of stale wine and long settled dust.

Gabriel made a quick decision, " I'm leaving the secret door ajar because this side is plain and whitewashed so it might take too much time to locate the mechanism. I have high hopes we'll be able to find the Heart of Stars, and run for it before our enemies become aware of us."

"Do you really think that's possible?" Toby was doubtful.

"We have to believe that, Come on, let's go and get it."

A short flight of steps led them up into the Butler's Pantry. Gabriel moved with silent stealth towards the only door, which he assumed would open into the kitchens. Toby and Daisy followed, quiet as mice, feeling their way as their eyes became accustomed to the gloom.

Gabriel was relieved to find the door unlocked, "Shush!" He put a finger to his lips to signal the need for silence as he led the way across the deserted kitchen with its wooden table and endless empty shelves. Nobody had cooked in the big cast iron ovens for decades. The fires had long been extinguished.

The servants' staircase, alive in times past with busy footmen carrying elaborate dishes to the banqueters, was as empty and forbidding as steps leading up to a gallows. With no idea what awaited them at the top, they paused for a moment to calm their racing hearts by breathing deeply and allowing the silent words of the Lumerinda to occupy their minds.

"Only the Lumerin can help us now," whispered Gabriel. "The moment has arrived." With one more deep breath, they tiptoed upwards towards the Great Hall.

The once magnificent room, now in disrepair, was hung with tapestries emblazoned with strange symbols. Black pillar candles, perched on iron sconces at intervals along the walls, flickered eerily. At the far end, to the left of the main entrance, a wooden platform had been constructed specially for the ceremony Maxwell Delano intended to perform just before midnight. On a black plinth in the centre of that platform stood the most incredible jewel, about three inches in diameter and bright as a Greening dawn. So far, the surrounding, sinister atmosphere, had completely failed to penetrate its flawless facets.

"Take a look at that!" Gabriel could scarcely believe his luck. "There's the Heart of Stars, unguarded, and just waiting to be rescued. Let's go!" Elated, they ran forward, hoping to grab it and make a quick exit back along the secret passage.

Then, it started, as though the world had gone into slow motion. Just four or five steps from their goal, Gabriel's legs began to buckle, as Toby and Daisy froze on the spot, unable to move, however hard they tried.

Feeling physically sick, Daisy began to hope that she would not throw up. Just behind her, a very dizzy Toby was trying hard not to fall over because the room was spinning like a merry-go-round. An uncomfortable pressure settled on the top of Gabriel's head, causing pain in his eyes and dulling his mind.

"Don't give in to it!" His voice sounded hoarse as he employed all his willpower to force it to work. "Think about us as a single, solid unit, think of us together and strong."

The door to the left of the platform opened, and for the first time since their arrival in Lumenor, Toby and Daisy found themselves in the all- encompassing, foul presence of Maxwell Delano, all decked out in a crimson robe, with the forbidding black star of his evil alliance adorning the centre of his chest. His thick, iron-grey hair looked impossibly neat and those eyes, like bottomless pits in his pallid skin, spoke of depths that should never be explored.

Daisy wanted to scream, but didn't have enough energy. Toby just stared, unable to avert his gaze, even though he was on the verge of passing out. Seven familiar Dark Stars had followed their leader into the hall.

Delano, who couldn't believe what he was seeing, flew into such a rage that his pale complexion turned almost the same colour as his robe. "They're supposed to be dead, Irina! You've lied to me! I gave you my trust and you've proved to be a useless waste of space!"

"They were seen on the boat - they drew the curtains, they must have turned in because they switched off the lights. Fifteen minutes before we set the explosion, Shade came back to report that they were still there. Nobody had left the boat so we all went back and blew it to smithereens."

Her voice had begun to rise with frustration and hurt pride before she became angry, answering Max back for the first time since she had known him. "And what about Hugo?" Irina demanded. "Hugo and Belladonna? They were supposed to make sure."

"It was your responsibility!" bellowed Max in absolute fury, refusing to let her off the hook.

Irina still perplexed that Hugo always got off so lightly, retaliated a second time.

"We have them now, don't we?" she was screaming at the top of her voice. "And that's thanks to the enchantments I've created in this room. The fools can't move."

Max, deciding to waste no more time on her, turned away to fix his attention on an unfortunate Sid Planks, who was leaning casually against the wall, enjoying the argument. Irina felt the rejection and backed off, choosing to ignore it for the time being, because it suited her ambition to make sure that she remained an important part of the midnight ceremony.

"Planks, you idiot!" Delano barked, fixing his victim with a drop-dead angry stare. "You've already been paid more than you deserve for a job that has been bungled. You're a walking disaster, so take your other two monkeys, get some rope, and tie this scum up before I send you to hell!" The black eyes flashed with all the force of a full on storm.

Sid Planks winced. He didn't like being called an idiot or a monkey one little bit, but since he had been paid more money than he had ever seen in his shifty life, he did as he was told with mounting resentment, vowing that when this was over, nobody would ever insult either him or his good mates again. He was going home tomorrow, anyway, and he wouldn't be needing the likes of Delano again any time soon.

Gabriel, Toby and Daisy, still unable to move, were dragged down the hall to three ornate dining chairs, which Barry Mackintosh had placed side by side. One by one, the captives were then securely bound to them at the wrists and ankles. As luck would have it, Barry did not know that he had placed those chairs just on the edge of the enchantments Irina had created to stop intruders from touching the Heart of Stars. Gabriel felt the life returning to his body, though the pressure on his head had eased only a little.

"As you can see," gloated Delano, "I have given you the best seats in the house, so you can look at your prize and realize that you can never win it. Your failure will bring despair, and your silly lanterns will soon turn black, driving you all mad. In about three hours, it's going to be all over for you, and then I will say what happens in Lumenor." The crazed expression on his face was terrifying. Toby and Daisy looked away, unable to cope with the malice and insanity. Summoning his courage, Gabriel needed all his willpower to contain the enemy's hatred in silence without holding on to it, or allowing himself to be shaken by its force.

"The seven stones, Greenway! Where are they?" The black holes narrowed to menacing slits.

"You can't seriously imagine that I'd tell you, even if I did know."

"No matter. When I've finished with you and your little friends, I'll be paying a visit to the Greenway estate to talk to the lovely Brigit and the rest of the family."

Gabriel felt the blood draining from his face, but refused to look away until Delano snapped his fingers as a signal for his accomplices to leave the room. Glowering one last time at the prisoners, he stormed out of the Great Hall in a whirl of puffed-up pride, slamming the heavy door behind him.

"What a relief he's gone." Daisy was trembling. "I'm freezing again and I still feel sick."

"It's like drowning in iced water," moaned Toby, "and all that crappy whispering in my head is getting worse again, as if this place were full of cruel people."

"It is Toby, though they're not yet visible," explained Gabriel, offering some reassurance. "I'm afraid that your talent for communication makes you particularly vulnerable to the atmosphere. If Daisy wasn't tied to the chair, she might be able to help you. Let's talk about our journey so far, and all the wonderful things we have experienced. Let's laugh at Dark Star's mess-ups... anything we can do to keep out the whispering and the cold, because the potions will have completely worn off by midnight. Daisy, just try to imagine sending some of your beautiful colours to Toby."

Surprisingly, Daisy's efforts did help Toby to keep his spirits up. Daisy was pleased to discover that she was still a Healer of Souls, even here sitting in the freezing cold on the rim of Hell. It was the longest three hours any of them had ever spent.

27 THE HEART OF STARS

Somehow, they survived the torture, though none of them knew how. They talked about places they had visited and the good friends they had made. They cracked jokes and took turns to invent funny rhymes and limericks.

"If I think about Ynys Arian and the sisters, I might be able to draw enough strength to send more colours to both of you," Daisy said, "here goes, I'll give it a try."

"It helps," Toby was grateful for her effort, "but still I can't totally shake of the attacks of the whispering shadows because they're getting stronger. Can't you hear them?" he pleaded. "They're telling me that I'm rubbish and that you two are laughing and turning against me."

"It's nonsense!" said Gabriel with absolute certainty, though he was fighting his own torture in the form of the crushing pressure on top of his head. "It's black light and it's all lies! They tell lies to destroy you! Think about how much we've been through together. We're family like the sisters of Arian. Raven Stone says that the three of us are bound together by a common destiny, stretching across time and space and that the full extent of that connection is too awesome to understand. How could we ever turn against you?"

The power of Gabriel's words dragged Toby back into the moment, enabling him to re-establish his connection so that he quickly received information of a very different kind. "I'm getting an idea now that we need to sing when Delano starts his corrupting incantations. Maybe we should sing the Lumerinda."

"No!" Daisy experienced sudden clarity, as an image of Rio appeared in her mind. "It's not that, it's the other one - yeah, the hymn Raven taught us that was so important - the Heartsong."

"Of course," agreed Gabriel, his face lighting up. "That's why the Lumerin insisted on it. It all makes sense now." He was thoughtful for a minute and then added, "But I'm certain that you two must sing, and that I must keep quiet, because the addition of my voice would create the wrong effect. This part of the task is your destiny, the reason you're here."

All discussions stopped when the door opened at exactly eleven thirty-five, Maxwell Delano's pale face bore a look of triumph as he cast a gloating eye over his captives, relishing their defeat a second time. A triumphant line of seven Dark Stars followed after him with Irina first, then Justin, Hugo and Belladonna in that order, with Sid, Jack and Barry bringing up the rear. They were now all dressed in the ceremonial crimson robes decorated with a single black star. Each one carried a tarnished, silver lantern lit by a black candle, which they placed, one by one, in a neat row before the magnificent Heart of Stars.

"What an insult!" murmured Daisy, "it's beginning to feel personal now, and that makes me determined to put up the fight of my life, whatever horrors those scumbags throw at me!" Then with fiery intent, she sent an extra dose of strong colours to Gabriel and Toby, who immediately picked up her mood, and mentally prepared for battle.

"Now, it begins!" hissed Delano, relishing his moment as the bringer of a Shadow Dawn, a corruption of all that the Order of Lumen held dear. It was a sweet taste of victory. "Take your positions - Irina to my left on the platform, and Justin to my right. Hugo, go and guard the main entrance with Belladonna."

A very miffed Hugo Shade took up position by the door, wondering why he hadn't been allowed a central place on the platform beside his hero Max. If the truth were told, he was both angry and hurt, but unable to object because it was almost time to begin.

Sid Planks and his mates, scarcely important enough to be a major part of anything, were dispatched to guard the back door by the servants' stairs. They were not in the least bit bothered, being keen to get it over with so they could go back to Robinswood and have a nice life on their dubious proceeds.

Toby, Daisy and Gabriel began to shiver again as the temperature dropped well below zero. It was so cold that their breath became visible and their lungs ached. Gabriel realized that his Lumerin potions had almost worn off. The time was exactly ten to midnight; soon, the clocks would chime for the Threshold celebrations of the year 2205.

"Now," said Delano, making the first small incantation to establish a connection to Dark Star. The shadows swirled around him like poisonous smoke, as the whispers attacking Toby became so real and so loud that Daisy and Gabriel could also hear them echoing around the empty hall.

Raising his arms, he began to chant, intoning the abominable words in a long forgotten language, a language that had no business to be used in front of the Heart of Stars… a language that had no business to be spoken at all. The empty voice droned on without emotion, like an echo of the pit it had come from.

The captives watched the darkness growing denser behind Delano, like an oil slick spreading out to pollute and choke all decent life. Vile faces were forming in the seething poisonous mass, vile faces with eyes like malicious frozen space. Dark Star had arrived to crush everyone who stood in its way.

Sid Planks was scared to death, as the spreading mass began to snake around the sides of the Great Hall, devouring the weak light from the black candles. It was true that he had been very well paid, but he definitely hadn't signed up for this, not in a month of Sundays. He would have run for it through the back door if his legs hadn't begun to feel like jelly. He couldn't have known that Irina's enchantments would also stop him from running out on Delano. He only knew that he was very afraid and that he didn't want to be in this place with these people anymore.

Toby began to slide back into whispering shadows as the empty droning voice continued the deadly invocation and the writhing tentacles of black light tried to penetrate his mind. Once more, Gabriel was almost paralyzed by the crushing pressure on his head, when he became aware of Daisy's sweet, high voice, hesitant at first, then growing in confidence, as the space around them rang with the pure notes of Ancient Lumen, the musical language of light. In an instant, the air began to shimmer like gold dust, releasing the pressure on Gabriel and bringing Toby back from the edge. Gabriel remembered something very important. He remembered two voices. "There must be two voices! Two voices! Sing, Toby! Sing!" Gabriel couldn't have cared less now whether Delano heard him or not. Then, recalling that the Order of Lumen everywhere were lighting up their lanterns, he concentrated on that image in order to tap into their strength.

With a supreme effort, Toby joined his voice to Daisy's, increasing in volume and fullness as the words of the Heartsong flowed through him in harmony with his cousin. The sound expanded, soaring like a choir, as if more than two people were singing.

Maxwell Delano, too far into the ceremony at this point, found himself powerless to stop them. To cease the incantation now would destroy his one chance to corrupt the Heart of Stars. Irina Slack and Justin Feral were also forced to maintain their places, at the risk of halting the summoning by causing a break in the line of energy between themselves and Max.

Hugo Shade moved away from the door, understanding that he was the only person left with the power to stop the singing, and his intention was to stop it forever. "Stay exactly where you are and do not move!" he ordered Belladonna as he ran towards the captives, only to find that he was reliving the experience of

The Sanctuary. As soon as he came into contact with the golden light, he was thrown backwards, landing in a crumpled, ungainly heap at Belladonna's feet.

By now, Sid, Jack and Barry were all frozen to the spot as Gabriel and the young ones had been earlier.

It had become a battle of voices, as Gabriel, unable to help, could only watch and continue to think about all the Lantern Ceremonies going on to back up Toby and Daisy. Delano droned on and on, louder and louder, fighting to take control. Picking up the Heart of Stars, he held it aloft, aiming his words directly into its centre. The jewel shone like the sun as the seeking darkness approached to eclipse its splendour and change the notes of the Great Song contained within it.

Toby and Daisy, strong from the blending of their efforts with Gabriel's steadfast presence and his link to the Order of Lumen, continued the ancient Heartsong of the bright stars, louder and bolder, filling the space above and around them with its rich tones.

Now the golden light was pouring into the centre of the Great Hall, cascading out to meet the twisting, infernal stream. The ropes binding Gabriel and the children firmly to their chairs began to dissolve, enabling them to break free. Toby and Daisy, moved by something they did not understand, stood up and linked hands. Freed from fear, they began to take slow, purposeful steps towards Maxwell Delano.

The dark incantation began to weaken as Delano's voice dried up and froze. The golden haze in the centre swirled itself into the fluid form of an exceptionally tall woman, stretching out her arms to protect Toby and Daisy who came to a halt and stopped singing. Max and his two helpers cowered on the platform. Toby remembered the conversation in his dream on their first night in Lumenor. It was the same Lumerin who had spoken to him so long ago, and now she had come to help, just as she had promised. The golden lady turned her attention directly to Maxwell Delano, her right arm outstretched with the palm facing towards him as she spoke. Her resonant voice reminded Toby of Rio, except that its tone was deeper and fuller, like a great bell.

"I am Aurora and this is my land!"

The Heart of Stars was pulled from Delano's hands by an unseen force so strong he could not resist. Gabriel ran forward, catching the jewel with skill as it flew towards him.

Aurora continued. "Maxwell Delano! I am here at the request of the two children you see before you. It was written long ago and now it is so. The Heart of Stars may not be destroyed. It is forbidden to interfere with the Great Song, and so, for your efforts, you are lost and must forfeit your right to existence in Lumenor. Your own kind may claim you, according to their law."

"Do something Hugo!" Belladonna screeched in desperation.

"I can't," a defeated Shade muttered in a small voice. "It's too late... we have to go. Trust me. I have orders from Max." Opening the door with a sudden, swift gesture, he grabbed her arm and dragged her into the gallery at the top of the grand staircase. "Now run!" he ordered. "Get out of here as fast as you can!"

Maxwell Delano began to groan as though in terrible pain.

"What's happening to me?" cried Irina as her hands became transparent. Justin was speechless with terror watching his legs begin to disappear. The hellish stream of leering shadows curled around all three, absorbing them little by little into the Dark Star... until not a trace remained. Delano was the last to go, still wailing like a banshee. The black mass spun like a Catherine wheel, smaller and denser, until it was sucked into itself like a dying sun collapsing into a black hole. Sid, Jack and Barry all fell heavily and lay unconscious on the floor.

Gabriel, holding the precious Heart of Stars, wept with shock and relief, bowing his head in the presence of Aurora. Toby and Daisy were now resting, enfolded in her arms, as the hall filled with golden Lumerin. The sky outside the windows came alive with Threshold fireworks. Aurora spoke again to Gabriel.

"Return my Heart to its rightful place. Your harp prophecy is now fulfilled and the influence of the Order of Lumen will spread across Lumenor. This quest is complete, Gabriel Greenway."

"Do you mean there might be another one?" Right at that moment, Gabriel hoped desperately that the answer was No.

There was no reply to that question as the sweet voices of the Lumerin filled the air and the form of Aurora merged with them. The tarnished silver lanterns with their black candles disintegrated into small heaps of dust and the temperature rose again, wiping out all memory and trace of Maxwell Delano.

"Oh, cheerio then…" Daisy was sobbing as she waved her goodbyes to the face of the Lady Aurora blending back into the golden light. "See you."

The Lumerin began to fade, leaving a delicious atmosphere behind them, and three very weary warriors.

28 THE HALL OF AWEN

Ignoring the three unconscious men, a dazed Gabriel Greenway slumped on the chair to which he had previously been tied. He held the Heart of Stars lovingly in both hands, looking into its mysterious pulsating depths. Daisy and Toby joined him, pulling their own chairs close to form a triangle and, waiting for what seemed like an age until Gabriel found his voice again.

"We've really done it," he said in disbelief. "It really is all over." It was going to be difficult to come to terms with things being normal again. "Thank you so much for coming to help us."

"We had to." Toby was matter of fact. "You discovered a prophecy, remember?"

"Destiny!" Daisy declared, pulling a face. "You, of all people, Gabriel, should know that - you mention it often enough. Anyway, we've had some fun along the way right? It hasn't all been terrible."

"And I can see that you've got your old cheek back!" Gabriel laughed. "I'm so glad about that."

The main door burst open, admitting Tristan Wilde, his cheeks pink from the chill weather. He rubbed his hands and blew on them.

"Saw the golden Lumerin from outside." He beamed at them. "Knew it was going to be the best Threshold ever. Must say though, you three look a bit worse for wear, but I'm so very glad to find you alive and kicking. Couldn't help worrying. I've come to take you back to Angelica's. You can go home tomorrow. Is that a relief, or what? I've brought extra sandwiches and a flask. You must be starving."

"I'm afraid that Hugo Shade and Belladonna Slack got away," Gabriel apologized to Tristan.

"I saw a black car leave the grounds, but there was nothing I could do. Don't suppose he'll have strength or power of any kind for a long time or even ever again, now that Aurora has paid us a visit and Delano's gone. All major Dark Stars involved in ceremonies, with the exception of Shade and Slack, have been absorbed tonight, and all pawns like Planks will have no memory of it at all. The Lumerin told me on their way out. Hugo and Belladonna haven't any pals so they won't be doing any summoning in the near future."

"Crazy Shady," said Daisy, "drove back into the darkness where he came from with poisonous Belladonna. Wonder if they'll get married?"

"Ultra gruesome!" Toby scowled and pretended to retch. "Trust you, Daise, to come up with something as revolting as that. A match made in hell, if you ask me."

Noticing the three men sleeping on the floor, Tristan nudged Sid Planks with the toe of his boot. Sid opened his mouth and began to snore loudly.

"Awful manners." Daisy put on her best superior scowl of disapproval.

"Certainly not dead, then." Tristan nudged him a second time before moving on to Jack and Barry.

"No," said Gabriel. "Aurora in her wisdom has let them off and given them a chance to change their ways. Apparently, they didn't really know what was going on or how terrifying it would be. They were just some local small time crooks lured in by Delano with a promise of big money. They appear to have been very frightened, but they're going to wake up feeling like they've had too much of a Threshold Celebration. They'll remember nothing about Dark Star or the Order of Lumen, but they'll be considerably better off. Do you know - I heard Delano say he'd paid them. How fortunate is that? And after all the trouble they've caused." He grimaced as Barry Mackintosh rolled over and joined in the snoring.

"Come on," said Tristan. "Let's get out of here. We've got what we came for. Sweet dreams, boys."

After one last look at the Great Hall, Gabriel, Toby and Daisy made their way down the grand staircase to the front door. The constellation of Harmony Wheel twinkled on the horizon as they tumbled out into the snow in the early hours of an incredible Threshold morning and the year 2205.

* * * *

And so it was, that twelve days later, Gabriel, Toby and Daisy boarded a boat to return the Heart of Stars and the seven jewels to Ynys yr Delyn, the place of the Golden Harp, across the Western Ocean, where the grey seals cry to the moon and the evening sun sets in a blaze of rosy violet and crimson glory.

"Ynys yr Delyn," dreamed Gabriel, "often just referred to as The Island, is our most important and sacred place, a place we must be before the fortieth day of Earthstill, which in our calendar, marks the return of the sun to the land. At this time, the lambing begins at Sylvanhay and new life will be born all over Lumenor."

"I wish I could have stayed for the lambing," said Toby, sorry to be missing something so important.

"Lambing comes every year, but this playing of the harp to welcome the sun with you in the Hall of Awen, is a unique event." He turned away so that the children could not see the pain creep into his eyes.

* * * *

The ice green winter sea, though choppy, wasn't turbulent

enough to make them feel sick. Grey seals appeared, bobbing in the water, calling to Toby to come and play in the waves.

Daisy looked at Gabriel, muttering through the wool scarf she had pulled right up to her nose. "Where d'you suppose Hugo Shade has gone?"

"Nobody has any information yet. As you know, he left with Belladonna Slack just before the Dark Star absorbed Maxwell Delano and he hasn't been seen since. Tristan Wilde has been given the job of tracking them down, but I doubt if they'll dare to show their faces for a very long time. The energy which Aurora and the gold Lumerin left behind will have blocked them out and left them powerless."

Daisy, satisfied with his answer, smiled with contentment as she stared into the deep green water lapping around the boat and listened to the freedom calls of the sea birds. A warm, pleasant sense of safety kept the cold out as she pondered for a while on the awful fate of Maxwell Delano.

"Delano got Dark Star, which is exactly what he wanted. Maybe some of the things we think we want are not always so good for us then."

Gabriel was waving at the lone figure of a man, waiting patiently on the harbour wall - a man who had never felt so happy to be alive as he did today.

"It's you... only old!" Toby was surprised to see the similarity between Gabriel and the stranger when the boat docked and he stepped off on to the jetty.

The older man did, indeed, bear a very strong resemblance to Gabriel, except that his once jet-black curls were streaked with silver, and the deeply bronzed face was somewhat weathered. However, those lively, velvet brown eyes, surrounded by deep laughter lines still retained that familiar Greenway twinkle.

"It's my father," said Gabriel much amused at the idea of his older self. Even now, at the age of sixty his father was considered to be quite a handsome man.

"Hector Greenway," announced the stranger, introducing himself to Toby and Daisy, who shook hands politely. "I'm

Gabriel's old dad and I'm the proudest man alive today." He threw his arms around his younger son with joy and relief. "I wish I could have helped you, boy." His voice held a tinge of regret, "but it was not permitted."

"I know. I had to go my own way and sort it out myself, but thankfully the connection proved to be strong and all the right people were provided at exactly the right time. It wasn't a walk in the park, as you can imagine, but we're all fine and I'd do the whole thing again if I had to."

"Let's hope that never happens."

Together they made their way to the Hall of Awen, a full twenty minutes on foot. There were no cars here, as the island was very small. Some people used bicycles, but most walked. The tall, single storey construction comprising the Hall of Awen itself and a library was an impressive building of solid, pink granite. Around it, smaller buildings of the same material housed visitors and some single residents. There were also meeting rooms, kitchens and a long dining room with oak tables. A vegetable garden and an orchard provided fresh produce for everyone. Beyond the compound lay a village, where families and fishermen lived. Everyone had a part to play in this special community.

An elderly woman dressed in the familiar, cobalt blue robe of the Order of Lumen stood at the entrance to the Hall of Awen, ready to greet her guests. Andromeda Harper was descended from the family who had played the Harp of Creation for longer than anyone could possibly remember.

"I rarely play these days," she told Daisy and Toby. "My daughter, Iola, now has that privilege and she will pass it on to her son Dylan, who, though he's the youngest of the children, has inherited the talent. Come, you must see it and the stones must be reset."

The Hall of Awen with its high, vaulted ceiling, contained arched, windows of stained glass decorated with scenes depicting the Lumerin. At the one end, it looked out across the sea towards Heartland and at the other towards Westernesse, so that the waves could be heard crashing on the white sandy shores from both directions. In the morning, the sunrise flooded through the east facing glass and then in the evening the reddening sunset blazed through the west.

On a low table beneath each window sat a gleaming silver lantern, decorated with leaves, flowers and birds in gold, and pastel hued enamels, to match a wide painted border circling the room. There was no other decoration on the whitewashed walls or rosy marbled floors but the effect was simple and stunning - a bright place with an atmosphere of quiet joy and great beauty.

The fabled harp sat on a circular, marble platform in the centre of the hall. Gilded chairs, upholstered in a soft sage green fabric, were arranged around it, in four tiers, of seven rows each. Toby checked the frame to see exactly where the stones were going to fit. Opening the belt bags they had carried for so long, Gabriel and the children carefully placed the seven stones on a cloth spread on the floor at the base of the harp. Then, the Heart of Stars, clear and sparkling like an exquisite diamond, was unwrapped from its thick felt covering to take its place alongside the others. The set of magical jewels was complete again.

Hector Greenway, with an air of solemn ceremony, slotted the stones back into place down the front frame, securing each one with a gentle twist as Andromeda stated its name.

"Peace and Inspiration... Protection... Good Health... Happiness... Love and Kindness... Wisdom... and Plenty. There, all together and home."

Finally, the stunning Heart of Stars shone once more in its rightful place, waiting for the harpist to make the instrument sing the notes of the Great Song again. When the crimson light of the setting sun flooded the west window with its dying glow, so the blue robed Order of Lumen filed into the Hall of Awen, singing the Lumerinda as Iola's skilled fingers moved nimbly across the strings to accompany them.

Toby and Daisy were so entranced that they forgot to sing. The seven stones began to pulsate with light, each according to its colour, and it seemed as though they were spinning outwards, almost as if you could see the notes as well as hear them. The Heart of Stars threw light up into the vaulted ceiling in all the colours of the spectrum. Just when the children thought that it couldn't get any better, the Lumerin arrived, dancing and singing around the hall, before zooming like flying rainbows into the lanterns under the windows.

The magic was now restored. Peace had been secured and the influence of the Harp of Creation would spread like ripples, magnified by its precious stones, to travel across the length and breadth of Lumenor, shaping the land and the lives of its people each and every time it was played. The quest was complete and it was time to rest.

29 THE UNICORN GATE

Around the table after the evening meal, as so often happens in the lull following a long period of action and excitement, Toby found himself wondering what life was going to be like now that all the danger was over.

"What's next then, Gabriel? What do you think destiny has in store for us now?"

"As you already know, there's an important party planned for the fortieth day of Earthstill to mark the return of the sun when new creatures are born and the first flowers open."

"You mean snowdrop, coltsfoot, crocus and celandine," said Daisy, showing off her knowledge of flowers.

Gabriel laughed, at her know-all expression. It was a part of her personality, which had become almost endearing.

"That's exactly what I mean," he answered. "Now, some of our old friends who are free to do so, will be coming here to take part in those celebrations."

He decided not to mention that those old friends would also be saying goodbye, because he could scarcely bear to think about Toby and Daisy leaving Lumenor. This powerful link of common destiny, which had pulled the children across time and space, would soon be sending them back to their own world. Gabriel vowed that he would not waste a single second of their precious remaining time together by moping about a certainty that could not be changed.

The fortieth day of Earthstill was a very happy one in the Hall of Awen as Toby and Daisy greeted the small group of old friends who had been able to make the journey to Ynys Yr Delyn. All of them had played a vital part in the quest for the Heart of Stars and in the defeat of Maxwell Delano.

Morag was the first to arrive, followed by Sage Flowers who, as Daisy observed, seemed completely over the moon to see Gabriel again. Next came Dion Hawke with Olivia, followed by Krishan and Kavita Sharma, then Michael Dory and Seren Shore. Daisy flew into loud exclamations of pleasure when she spied the most gorgeous ring that Michael had ever made sparkling on Seren's delicate finger. She spent ages admiring it and much to Toby's disgust, going on and on about weddings. Finally, there was Tristan Wilde, jovial as ever, but still searching for Hugo Shade and Belladonna Slack in his spare time.

The happy reunion continued over lunch and throughout the afternoon, then Morag spoke to Gabriel just as the sun began to set.

"It's time now, Gabriel. It's time for their return. You have to tell them."

Before everyone went to change for the Lantern Ceremony, Gabriel spoke quietly to Toby and Daisy.

"Your old clothes are in your rooms, the ones you discarded during the hot weather," he said. "Olivia and Dion have brought them from Oaklands, and you're required to wear them for the Lantern Ceremony."

"Oh, d'you mean we are going back?" cried Daisy, understanding immediately. "Going back tonight?"

Toby, too choked to speak, squinted at Gabriel through a veil of welling tears. Gabriel put an arm around each of them.

"Sorry to keep mentioning it," he said, his voice breaking with emotion, "but it's that old word - destiny. You were only lent to us for one special reason, you see, and the mission is now over. Apart from that, I'm in no doubt that there's still so much for you to do in the world you came from. I'm afraid that your departure can't be avoided or even delayed, though right now, I can scarcely imagine life without you. I was once more nervous about looking after two eleven year olds than facing Delano, but that experience has been, as you say… Epic?"

"I wasn't sure if our world still existed," Toby sighed, torn between sudden memories of his own family and his wonderful friend Gabriel, to whom he was much attached.

"All worlds exist in their own time and space Toby. Sometimes, they're linked by bridges or gateways that may allow access in very special circumstances and only ever at the right time."

"There's something important, Gabriel, something Morag said on that first night in Lumenor. "Never forget Toby, it is love that opens all the right doors." Gabriel nodded in approval.

Returning to her room and collecting her skinny jeans and butterfly tunic from the chair, Daisy was surprised to discover that they were blue again. How bright that red waterproof jacket and trainers looked compared to the more sober stuff she had whinged about but got used to. During this precious time in Lumenor, the colours inside her and the wonderful company of true friends had become altogether much more important to Daisy than wearing the latest fashions.

Dressed in their old things, Toby and Daisy were shown to reserved places in the Hall of Awen by Hector Greenway. They had the best seats directly in front of the Harp of Creation, with a perfect view of the Heart of Stars and the seven jewels. Gabriel was given the chair between them so that he could link hands with each one.

Then robed in the traditional white wool of her craft, Iola Harper began to strum the melody of the Lumerinda, prompting everyone to stand. All were looking at Toby and Daisy and some were tearful. When the music soared to a crescendo and the bright stream of Lumerin filled the room, Daisy and Toby were surprised that they could no longer feel the firm grip of Gabriel's hand, as they became light headed and began to float. It was a sensation like drifting into a gentle dream. Little by little, the rosy, marbled Hall of Awen, the golden Harp of Creation with its glowing jewels and the blue robed Order of Lumen began to melt and fade, until there was only music and light and then unconsciousness.

When they awoke, they were lying on the mossy floor of a frosty, woodland clearing. Carpets of white snowdrops had replaced the bluebells.

"It's a winter's day here," said Toby realizing that they had somehow been returned to the Dreaming Forest.

"Look, there's Rio!" Daisy spied their old friend, the unicorn, trotting towards them through the trees.

"Follow me." The unicorn invited, in silver bells and disco colours, as he took the pathway meandering immediately to the right. "It is time you were going home."

"Will we ever be able to come here again?" Toby's mind was still firmly fixed on Gabriel and the Order of Lumen.

"Who knows where you will go, or indeed, when?" Rio answered. "You are experienced travellers, you have walked between worlds and you have done a great thing for Lumenor. Only time will answer your question - and as ever the strength of your connection and then, of course, destiny,"

Soon, they arrived at a familiar mint green door set back in a red brick wall where the trees ended. Rio touched their foreheads one final time as they took up their positions in front of it. First, they heard the rushing of cool air coupled with a spinning sensation and then the blaring sound of modern traffic, as they found themselves once again on the wide pavement of a busy road, in front of a park, on the outskirts of London. The clouds had completely cleared to release the sun and the dark green trees looked heavy with late summer foliage. The pelican crossing beeped loudly as six pedestrians crossed to the other side of the road.

Toby checked his watch, which was now working and read 11:54 15 AUG. It was a shock. "According to this, Daise, we've only been gone fifty-four minutes!"

"Totally impossible." Daisy frowned in complete disbelief,

"that's only six minutes for each one of the nine months we've spent in Lumenor."

The two of them were silent, trying to adjust to the idea of this uncanny time difference, and the deafening noise of a continuous stream of traffic, which seemed to be travelling at ridiculous speed. The sharp, persistent sound of Toby's mobile ringing in his pocket caused a moment of surprise. He pulled out the familiar smart phone to answer the call. "Hey, Mum."

"I thought you'd have been home by now," Rosa Malone complained "I was beginning to worry."

"I'm really sorry." Toby was so pleased to hear his mother's voice again. "You see, there was a hail storm and then we bumped into a few very good friends, and it all got so interesting, we kind of forgot what time it was."

"What hail storm?" she asked, puzzled.

"Never mind," Toby rapidly changed the subject. "We haven't got the bread yet, but we're almost at the shops so we'll be home in about twenty minutes."

"See you soon. Oh, and by the way, I've just had a call from your Auntie Grace. She says that Uncle Rob's been offered a great new job and he starts work the week after next. I know that'll cheer Daisy up because she's been so worried about the future."

As the good news from home was duly passed on to a very happy Daisy, the familiar stone unicorn who now had a name, continued his silent vigil from the wall above the peeling green door. For one brief moment, Toby thought he saw the statue wink at him.

THE END

ABOUT THE AUTHOR

Iona Jenkins worked as a teacher before changing career to become a counsellor/psychotherapist, mentor and life coach with both young people and adults in London. Her love of nature developed during her own imaginative childhood in a Yorkshire village. Growing up in a mining family, the young Iona loved exploring, discovering special places in all seasons and finding new creative ideas amongst the woods, fields, streams and even colliery wasteland in the countryside around her home. Today, Iona lives and writes amongst the magical landscapes of Wales where she is now working on the second Toby and Daisy adventure in the Legends of Lumenor series.

www.ionajenkins.com

Printed in Great Britain
by Amazon